THE SHOW
TO END ALL
SHOWS

ALSO BY CARY FAGAN

THE SHOW TO END ALL

SHOWS

MASTER MELVILLE'S MEDICINE SHOW BOOK TWO

CARY FAGAN

PUFFIN

an imprint of Penguin Canada Books Inc., a Penguin Random House Company

Published by the Penguin Group
Penguin Canada Books Inc., 90 Eglinton Avenue East, Suite 700, Toronto, Ontario, Canada M4P 2Y3

Penguin Group (USA) Inc., 375 Hudson Street, New York, New York 10014, U.S.A.
Penguin Books Ltd, 80 Strand, London WC2R 0RL, England
Penguin Ireland, 25 St Stephen's Green, Dublin 2, Ireland (a division of Penguin Books Ltd)
Penguin Group (Australia), 707 Collins Street, Melbourne, Victoria 3008, Australia
(a division of Pearson Australia Group Pty Ltd)
Penguin Books India Pvt Ltd, 11 Community Centre, Panchsheel Park, New Delhi — 110 017, India
Penguin Group (NZ), 67 Apollo Drive, Rosedale, Auckland 0632, New Zealand
(a division of Pearson New Zealand Ltd)
Penguin Books (South Africa) (Pty) Ltd, 24 Sturdee Avenue, Rosebank, Johannesburg 2196, South Africa

Penguin Books Ltd, Registered Offices: 80 Strand, London WC2R 0RL, England

First published 2014

1 2 3 4 5 6 7 8 9 10   (RRD)

LIBRARY AND ARCHIVES CANADA CATALOGUING IN PUBLICATION
Fagan, Cary, author
The show to end all shows / Cary Fagan.
(Master Melville's medicine show)

ISBN 978-0-670-06586-8 (bound)

I. Title. II. Series: Fagan, Cary. Master Melville's medicine show.

PS8561.A375S46 2014   jC813'.54   C2013-905140-6

Visit the Penguin Canada website at **www.penguin.ca**

Special and corporate bulk purchase rates available; please see
www.penguin.ca/corporatesales or call 1-800-810-3104, ext. 2477.

To all jugglers, magicians, acrobats,
and other practitioners of the "minor arts,"
amateur or professional, young or old

CONTENTS

MOST OTHER PERFORMERS CAN MANAGE

TO COVER UP AN ERROR,

BUT DROPPED OBJECTS SPEAK FOR THEMSELVES.

⤜ Marcello Truzzi ⤛

H̹E stood in front of the Stardust Home for Old
People. He had walked from very far away and it had
taken a long time, but finally he was home again. He
opened the door and saw people he recognized—old
Elsa Fargo and her sister, Rita Cooley, playing cards;
Mr. Macafee in his wheelchair doing the newspaper
crossword puzzle. Nobody paid Sullivan any attention
so he walked through the house to the stairs and up to
the third floor where his family had their apartment.
He saw his father sitting in an easy chair knitting a
sweater while his mother did the account books.

"We're turning a good profit these days," his mother said. "It's so much easier with one less mouth to feed."

"True," said his father, softly clicking the knitting needles. "Still, I miss Sullivan sometimes."

"Yes, I do too. But not as much as last month. Or the month before."

"No," his father agreed. "Not as much. Soon we won't even remember him."

Why were they saying such awful things? Why didn't they look up at him? Where was his sister, Jinny? Where was their friend Manny Morgenstern? He had to do something so they would look at him— had to stamp his feet or shout or scream. But when he tried, he couldn't move, couldn't get a sound out of his throat. He tried once more, tried as hard as he could to scream—

"Uhh!"

Sullivan sat up. It was dark and cold. He had thrown off the thin blanket. He could feel the jostling of the caravan as it moved along, pulled by the steady hoof-beats of Soggy Biscuit.

Every night lately, Sullivan had experienced the most vivid dreams. If it was a bad dream, the dark mood could linger miserably for hours after. And if it was a good dream, then the feeling was hard to let go and he felt sad when it faded. Lying in the dark now,

Sullivan felt the dream was both good and bad. It had left him feeling bereft and lonely. But at the same time he had been glad to see the Stardust Home and the people he knew, especially his parents. He wished that he could have "seen" Jinny and Manny, too.

Instead he was here, on a thin mattress, listening to the soft breathing of the others as the caravan moved through the night. They were on to another destination, to set up once more, and make meals, and clean up, and mend their things, and perform again. He had been kidnapped in the late spring. They had travelled through the long, hot summer, and now it was the fall, which meant that he had been part of the medicine show for a good five months. Right now this life seemed more real than the one he kept dreaming about.

Sullivan lay down again, pulling up the covers. He needed to get to sleep. Maybe he could dream something nice about home. He closed his eyes—and felt the caravan creak to a halt.

He opened his eyes again. Why had they stopped? He knew it was still the middle of the night because no light was slipping through the few thin cracks in the caravan walls. Maybe they were giving Soggy Biscuit a rest, although it was doubtful since they rarely showed the horse any kindness. Sullivan heard the twang of the seat springs up front, which meant that somebody was getting down. He heard them twang again, and then the sound of muffled voices. A moment later came the scraping of the key in the lock. Sullivan closed his eyes and turned his face to the wall.

He heard the back door of the caravan open. The flickering of lantern light played over his eyelids, but he didn't move.

"You see, my rose blossom? They're all sleeping like little lambs. I told you that there was nothing to worry about."

"You never think there's anything to worry about. If I had listened to you, I wouldn't have caught the girl trying to escape, would I?"

"True, absolutely true. That was quick and clever of you, to be sure. But it was three weeks ago, and after what we did to punish the poor child, I'm sure nobody else would dare try."

"What *we* did? What I did, you mean. You didn't have the stomach for it."

"I'm a weak man and I admit it. That only makes me more in awe of your great inner strength, my Amazon beauty. If you don't mind my making a suggestion, we ought to be on our way. As the poet once said, we've got miles to go . . ."

"And what if this is all for nothing? What if it never existed? What if it was found already?"

"Such negative thinking, my dear. I've done my research, and the secret went to their graves. But we shall find it."

"You're not half as clever as you think. You're not half as *anything.*"

"I'm sure you're right, my lollipop. It's a wonder you put up with me at all."

"Do shut up. And lock the door."

Sullivan heard the door close, heard the lock clank shut. Outside, Soggy whinnied. The whip cracked and the caravan's wheels began to turn again. He lay in the dark, not able to sleep, but it was a few minutes before he realized that someone else was awake too. He heard the muffled sound of crying.

The caravan had four low bunks that folded out from the walls, two lined up on one side and two on the other. His was on the left side of the door and farther back; the crying came from the right side, farther up. That meant Esmeralda. He pushed aside his blanket and crept so as not to wake Frederick or Clarence, although Clarence's two dogs thumped their tails.

Sullivan crouched by Esmeralda's bed and whispered, "Are you okay, Essy? Can I do something?"

He could just see the outline of her blanket, which covered her face. But she reached out a hand and Sullivan took it in his. She squeezed his fingers.

"It's nothing," she said in a small voice. "It's just that I heard them talking and, well, I know it was almost a month ago but it feels like it just happened."

Sullivan understood how she felt. He had once tried to escape in the night, only to be caught again. But Esmeralda had been even more bold. She had simply walked off in the middle of the day. After all, she had told Sullivan, it wasn't as if they were chained to the caravan. What was really stopping them from just leaving? So she had walked into the woods.

"Maybe it would help if you told me what happened." Esmeralda hadn't yet been able to talk about it.

"I don't know if I can."

"Just start at the beginning."

"All right, I'll try." She sat up in her bunk and took a slow breath. "I started running through the woods. Then I came to a road and I walked down it until I reached a house. It was a lovely little house with a garden. I knew nice people had to live there. I knocked on the door and these two elderly women opened it. They must have been sisters. They made me come inside and they gave me a bowl of wonderful potato soup, and I told them how I had been kidnapped and was running away."

Someone stirred. It was Clarence turning in his

sleep. Esmeralda continued in a low voice. "They said it was terrible that I'd had such a traumatic experience. They wanted to run me a nice hot bath and call the police. They told me I was safe."

"A bath! You must have been so glad to have found them."

"I started to cry something awful. Because I was happy. And I was going to rescue all of you. I wasn't going to forget. But just then somebody knocked at the door."

"Oh no. The Black Death."

"Yes, Mistress Melville. With a kerchief on her head and a shawl around her shoulders. She said that she was looking for her daughter who had run away. Her daughter was sick, she said. She forgot who her own mother was. She told lies. She was a danger to herself. Of course the two sisters got very upset. The Black Death put her arms around me and pretended to cry and thanked heaven that she had found me."

"But you must have told them she was lying."

"Of course. Maybe it was because I got so upset and angry and I screamed that she was an evil witch, but they believed her instead of me. I guess they trusted an adult more. Really I think they were just confused, and so when Mistress dragged me out of the house, they didn't interfere. She twisted my arm behind my back

and put her cold hand over my mouth so I couldn't scream. She dragged me all the way to the caravan."

Sullivan had seen them return. Everybody had. Mistress Melville had been furious, but Esmeralda had been so limp it looked like she might collapse. Then Mistress had locked Esmeralda into the Vanishing Box. For *eight* hours. Esmeralda must have felt as if she were trapped in a coffin.

Esmeralda began to cry again.

"It's okay, Essy," Sullivan said. "At least you have us. We're your friends. We all . . . we all love you."

"I know." She reached out to give Sullivan a hug. "Thank you. Now you go back to your own bed. You'll be exhausted tomorrow. We'll both be. And we still have to perform. Good night."

"Good night, Essy."

Sullivan made his way back to his bunk and lay down again. He was cold enough for his teeth to chatter and he pulled the thin blanket up to his chin.

✳ 2 ✳

A MEETING IN CHOOCHOOVILLE

NORVAL Simick poured some granola into a bowl, added milk, and began to crunch thoughtfully. He had studied for his science test, his backpack was packed, and in another ten minutes he'd head out to Beanfield Middle School. But he wasn't thinking about the test. He was thinking about the Sullivan Mintz Celebration Day.

Norval and Samuel Patinsky, his co-conspirator, as Principal Washburb had called him, had sure gotten in trouble for holding the celebration without permission at the end of the last school year. They had taken over the auditorium stage, hanging an enormous banner. They had put on dance music and had made declarations over the loudspeaker. The students had loved it and had even danced wildly—at least until Mr. Washburb had made the janitor shut down the electrical power.

The Celebration Day had been worth a week of detentions. Before that, Norval had been feeling pretty depressed about Sullivan's disappearance, especially after the police said that he had drowned in the Hasberg River. It had felt as if Sullivan would be quickly forgotten, but the Celebration Day reminded everybody of his friend's time at the school, even people who hadn't known him, which was most of the students, to be honest. What's more, it put Norval on the map. His buzz of good feeling lingered for days after as kids gave him the high-five, or slapped him on the back. He worried, though, about taking advantage of Sullivan's memory to make himself look good.

All that had happened right before the summer holidays. Now a new school year was almost two months old, the leaves were falling from the trees, and once more the memory of Sullivan was fading away.

These dreary thoughts spoiled Norval's appetite and he pushed his bowl away.

His mother came in dressed for work, picked up a

bagel, and took a bite even as she began to flip through the *Beanfield Gazette*. His dad came in next, fixing his tie.

"Oh dear," his mother said, leaning against the counter as she held up the paper.

"Don't tell me," said his father, pouring himself a coffee. "Are they expecting a bad bean crop this year?"

"It's a new poem by the Bard of Beanfield."

"Ah. Dreary is it?"

"Just awful. But can you blame her? I don't know what I'd do if anything happened to Norval."

"Nothing's going to happen." His father ruffled Norval's already unruly hair. "I hope, Norval, that you're feeling a little better this year. It's hard, losing someone you care about. But in the end, all you can do is accept it."

"Look at the time!" His mother snatched up her briefcase. "I'll see you both at dinner."

"I've got to go too," his father said. "Remember to lock up behind you."

"I always do," Norval called after them.

He heard the front door close. Immediately he grabbed the newspaper and began hunting for the poem. He knew that the Bard of Beanfield was Mrs. Mintz. Everybody knew. She used to write these quirky, funny, and sometimes just plain weird poems. But after

Sullivan had disappeared, the poems had disappeared too. And then about a month ago they had started up again, only they weren't the same.

Norval read the new poem.

I had a glass of water,
It was a lovely thing.
So pure and clear and perfect
It made me want to sing.

But in a careless moment
I knocked the glass about.
It rocked and shook and tipped right over
And poured the water out.

Where has that lovely water gone?
I ask with sigh and moan.
To what dark river has it run
To leave me all alone?

It was a strange poem, Norval thought. Who would bother to write about an ordinary glass of water? And why would someone get so upset about spilling it? And yet there was something so melancholy in the words. Norval knew that a poem could seem to say one thing when it was really saying something else. Because—so his English teacher had once told them—sometimes things were too painful, or simply impossible to express directly. No, Norval realized, the poem wasn't about a glass of water. It was about how sad Mrs. Mintz felt to lose her son.

Norval looked at the wall clock and realized that he should have already left for school. He threw on his backpack and grabbed his skateboard to make up for lost time. Norval must have been the last kid in school to want a skateboard. He had seen other kids zipping around on them but considered himself too uncoordinated even to try. He imagined himself falling backward or toppling over a curb while a line of cute girls laughed at him. It was Samuel who had convinced him that he could learn to skate.

"You don't have to do ollies or grinds or rock 'n' rolls," Samuel had told him.

"Good," Norval had replied. "Because I don't even know what they are."

Norval was amazed at how fun skating was. It was definitely a plus to have a friend like Samuel, someone who wasn't just like you. Now he moved quickly down the sidewalk, careful to slow down when he came near a pedestrian. He got to the schoolyard in record time, where he saw Samuel approaching on his own skateboard.

"Hey man, nice wheels," Samuel said.

"They ought to be. You made me use up all my savings to get them. Going in?"

"No, Norval, I think I'll stay out here all day and watch the sun set. Of course I'm going in."

They picked up their boards and began walking to the doors. "So, I've been thinking," Norval began.

"Oh no. Whenever you start thinking, I end up in trouble. I promised my parents that this year I wasn't going to have one black mark on my record."

"You used to be pretty good at getting into trouble without my help," Norval said. "I've been thinking about Sullivan's family. You know, his parents. We should go over to their house."

"That sounds awkward. Why?"

"Maybe we can help somehow. Just to make them feel a little better. We could go after dinner tonight."

"You sure know how to have a good time, Norval. Yeah, let's visit the dead kid's parents. Maybe they'll give us his old toys."

"That's okay, you don't have to come."

"Sure, make me feel guilty. I'll come. But if Sullivan's mother tries to hug us, I'm getting out of there."

When Norval and Samuel went to the Stardust Home that evening, they discovered that the Mintzes had gone out of town for two days. They had gone to a town called Choochooville.

The police might have believed that Sullivan was dead, but his family definitely did not. And his sister, Jinny, was sure that his disappearance had something to do with the strange travelling show the two of them had seen together. That Sullivan, who loved to juggle, had disappeared shortly after, along with his juggling equipment, seemed like the best—the only—lead that they had.

The trip that Gilbert and Loretta were on was the result of an advertisement they had placed in community newspapers all over the country.

— HAVE YOU LOST YOUR CHILD? — DID HE OR SHE LIKE TO DO MAGIC TRICKS, OR WALK ON A TIGHTROPE, OR PERFORM IN SOME OTHER WAY?

The Mintzes didn't have a computer so they had put the address of the Stardust Home at the bottom. And within a week the letters had started to arrive.

Many of them, however, were not what they had expected.

We have lost our daughter. She is fifty-seven years old. We are pretty sure that she has moved to Japan.

Are you also looking for stray animals? Our pig, Daisy, fell off the back of our truck . . .

Lost? We can't even get our son to move out. He graduated from college seven years ago and hasn't started looking for a job . . .

In all, seventy-two letters arrived at the Stardust Home. And while sixty-nine of them didn't match the circumstances of Sullivan's disappearance, three of them did. And three was exactly the number of children that Jinny said she and her brother had seen perform on that caravan stage. That meant three other families who might be in the same situation as the Mintzes, whose children might be with Sullivan at that very moment.

It was Loretta's idea to hold a meeting of these parents, along with Manny and Jinny. So Gilbert had taken out a map and they had looked for a town that was as close to everyone as possible. And that town was Choochooville.

The story of the town of Choochooville was told on a cast-iron plaque outside the jail. It explained how, nearly a hundred years ago, a local businessman had started a factory to manufacture the Choochoo Bar—a chocolate bar with a picture of a steam engine on it.

It so happened that the Choochoo Bar was Jinny Mintz's favourite kind. At that moment, she sat on a plastic stacking chair eating her third Choochoo Bar. The grown-ups were raising their voices and inter-rupting one another. They had put the chairs in a circle. Jinny, who was six, and Manny Morgenstern, who was eighty-one, sat with Gilbert and Loretta. Manny was not only a resident of the Stardust Home for Old People, he was also a close family friend. It was Manny who had agreed to go on the road with Jinny to search for Sullivan in order to stop her from running away to look by herself. They had been away now almost as long as Sullivan had been gone.

The rest of the people in the circle were adults. There were Emilio and Maria Samartino, whose son had disappeared along with his two small dogs. There were Ellen Raskin and Ann Whitford, the parents of a girl with red hair who had taken ballet and taught herself how to walk across a rope tied between two trees.

Finally, there was Horace Berliner. Horace Berliner was bald except for tufts behind his ears. He had cigarette ash on his worn-out army jacket and he sat back in his chair with his hands on his belly and looked half asleep. *He* wasn't raising his voice.

"Mr. Berliner," said Ellen Raskin. "You're the only one who hasn't expressed an opinion. Do you think your son is still alive?"

Horace Berliner blinked his eyes and sat up. He took out a handkerchief and noisily blew his large, cratered nose. "First of all," he sniffed, "he's not my son. He was an orphan and I took him in out of the generosity of my good nature. I'm his uncle. He grew up nice and strong, but he was sullen and difficult. Never liked to do any hard chores. When I wasn't watching, he'd start practising some magic trick or other. I don't know if the boy's alive, but if he is, I want him back. Then I'll show him what happens to an ingrate who runs away."

His speech silenced everyone else. Even Jinny stopped chewing. At last Manny said, "As I've tried to explain, Mr. Berliner, I don't think your nephew ran away. Or any of the others. Or that they were drowned or fell into a canyon or died some other way. I believe they were kidnapped."

"The ways that our kids disappeared do seem similar," said Mr. Samartino, pressing a handkerchief to his damp forehead. "But you haven't found any more clues. It's starting to feel as if you are chasing a phantom." Mr. Samartino stopped talking. His own words had been painful to say, and now his wife took his hand to comfort him.

"I understand those feelings," said Ann Whitford. "We're all so grateful that Manny and Jinny have been looking for the children. But time keeps passing. We were just starting to accept the loss of our daughter and get our lives back. Now we feel lost again. I know your motives are the best, Manny. But we're all going through a lot of suffering. Our hearts are crushed every day that our kids aren't found. I don't know how long we can take it."

Ellen Raskin put her hand on Ann's arm.

Jinny looked from one adult to the next. The meeting was definitely not going the way she had imagined. She had expected that the other parents would treat her and Manny like heroes. And now they wanted to give up. But those kids were out there somewhere—Jinny was sure of it.

She stood up.

She stamped her foot.

The adults stared at her.

"Grown-ups can be *so* disappointing," she declared. "Let me tell exaply what I saw at that medicine show.

I saw a piperope walker who was pretty and had long red hair and freckles. Everything she did was elegant, like a ballerina. But funny at the same time. She wore a lot of ribbons."

Ellen Raskin put her hand to her mouth. "That does sound like Louise."

"I saw a boy with two dogs," Jinny went on. "He was small. And he had big brown eyes. When he walked, he did a tip-to-one-side, tip-to-the-other. And one of the dogs had a brown spot on its nose and the other had a brown spot on its bum."

"Matthew walked just like that," Mrs. Samartino said, her voice choking.

"Those are just like his dogs," nodded her husband.

"The boy magician, he was kind of skinny and tall. But, you know, handsome. His hair fell over his eyes. He liked to flick his head back to get the hair away."

Mr. Berliner took an old toothpick from his pocket and put it between his teeth. "I always told Oscar he needed a haircut. But he liked looking at himself in the mirror too much."

For a while nobody said anything. Gilbert and Loretta stood up and put their arms around their daughter. At last Ellen Raskin got up and walked over to Jinny. She crouched down so that she could look directly into the girl's eyes.

"You're a very, very observant girl. And a smart one. Your brother is very lucky to have you for his sister."

"I know. That's the first thing I'm going to tell him."

Ellen Raskin smiled. "I believe you. I believe that our daughter is out there somewhere. And I want to know, Jinny, what we can do to help."

Jinny smiled. "You can give us money."

"Jinny!" exclaimed her mother.

"Well, we need some," Jinny insisted. "It's getting too cold to sleep in a tent every night."

"I would think so," Ellen said. "We have some savings. I definitely think we can manage some hotels."

"But maybe we should do more," said Ann Whitford. "Take a leave from our jobs. Take your place searching—"

"No!" Jinny almost screamed the word. "No, no, no! Manny and I are the ones who started. I'm the one who saw the medicine show. It would be bad luck if anyone else took over. I know it."

"You *have* been away a long time already," her father said gently. "You're a brave girl. But you should be home. You should be in school."

"I'm learning to read!" Jinny cried. "I can count and I can add and I can take away. I know where lots of countries are on the map. I know why rain falls and who flew the first airplane. Manny teaches me all the time. And we go into libraries and museums. Just the other day we were in a snow globe museum."

"That's wonderful, sweetheart," said her mother. "But wouldn't you like to be back in your own room and sleeping in your own bed?"

"Double no! Triple no! Not until I find Sullivan. You can't keep me home. I'll go looking by myself."

Jinny crossed her arms and planted her feet, as if to show she couldn't be moved. The adults looked at her burning eyes, her mouth tightly closed.

Mr. Samartino stood up and rubbed his face with his hand. "I trust you, Jinny. Something tells me that we should listen to you."

"Yes, yes," said his wife. "The little girl has something special about her. I think if anyone will find the children, she will."

Loretta and Gilbert looked at one another. Loretta's eyes teared up. "All right, for a while longer," she said. "But if you don't find anything—"

"If we don't find anything," Jinny said, "you can paint us blue and shoot us from a cannon."

"I don't think that will be necessary," said her father.

Mrs. Samartino smiled. "We have a big family. Cousins all over. We can give you their addresses. If you are ever nearby, you can stay with them. They'll treat you just like family."

"That's very kind of you," Manny said. "And I'm glad that we're all united on this. I think it's important that we have your support. Mr. Berliner? I expect that you'd like to help in some way."

Horace Berliner was cleaning his nails with a pocket knife. He clicked the blade closed and slipped it into his pocket. "If you're looking for a handout from me, you're not going to get it. For all I know, this is some sort of scam to get my money."

"It doesn't have to be money," Manny said.

"Tell you what. If you do manage to bring that good-for-nothing boy home, I promise to go easy on him. And now it looks to me as if this meeting is adjourned."

The man rose, hitched up his trousers, and walked across the room. He opened the door and let it shut again behind him without looking back.

"I don't like him much," Jinny said.

"Children say what grown-ups can't," noted Ellen Raskin.

"How about we all go to the restaurant for a good meal?" Loretta suggested, taking Jinny's hand. "We need to fill up these intrepid searchers before they go on their way."

"And we need to buy more Choochoo Bars," Jinny said.

Loretta picked Jinny up and gave her a smothering hug. Jinny giggled.

"Me next," said her father.

THE MAN IN THE SECOND ROW

"**C**AN it get any worse?" Master Melville asked.

They were having dinner in about the ugliest place they had ever set up camp, the parking lot of an abandoned used-car dealership. There was cracked concrete under Sullivan's feet. The nearby dealership office was boarded up and had a foreclosure notice tacked on the door. But for some reason, Master Melville had insisted on staying there. They had laid the table and made their dinner—not one of their usual culinary delights but instead baked beans and hot dogs.

"No, it can't get much worse than this place," Clarence answered.

"I did not mean this place." Master Melville's face had grown more gaunt, which the narrow beard he now scratched did not hide, although his moustache looked even longer. He spoke in a near whisper, as if—Sullivan thought—to stop himself from shouting. "I mean the show. And no, it cannot get worse. The performances have become sloppy. Joyless. You are robbing the audiences of the escape and pleasure they deserve. Do you know how I can tell? By the number of Hop-Hop Drops sold afterward. Do you know how many we sold yesterday? *Eight.* That is a new record, ladies and gentlemen, an all-time low. If you are wondering why we are having such a meagre repast this evening, now you know. Because I did not have the money to buy us anything better. We're lucky to be eating at all. The show has become lax, it has become joyless—"

"You are repeating yourself," Mistress Melville said dryly.

"You are right, my rare orchid. Thank you for pointing that out. Because it is only by having our faults pointed out to us that we can hope to improve. And you, young people, need a good deal of improving. I know we have had our dark moments lately"—Master

Melville gave Esmeralda a sympathetic look—"but you are not ordinary children. Therefore, I expect something more than ordinary efforts. Surely, you wish to take some pride in your performance. You must feel the honour of your profession, the noble calling of the entertainer, the thespian, the troubadour—"

"Now *you* are becoming pathetic," Mistress said, staring with distaste at the dinner on her plate. "Let *me* make the situation absolutely clear. If you four snot-nosed amateurs don't smarten up, things are going to get very bad around here. You are unhappy now? Then just wait. You know that I don't make idle threats. You, boy, the one who juggles. I have something for you."

Mistress never did remember Sullivan's name, not even the stage name that the Melvilles had given him. She reached into a bag that had been slung on her chair and pulled out three eggs. She placed them on the table in front of him.

"They're eggs," Sullivan said.

"Aren't you the clever one in the class."

"Are they real?"

"They're real and they're raw. And tonight you are going to juggle them."

"What a splendid idea!" cried Master Melville. "That ought to shake things up!"

"Juggle eggs? But I haven't practised."

"Then you'd better be a quick learner." Mistress speared a hot dog with her fork. "And now let us eat this revolting dinner in silence."

They didn't speak for the rest of the meal or during the cleaning up afterward.

The performers made their final preparations for the evening. As he got his props ready, Sullivan thought how just a few weeks ago, he had been glad to be part of the medicine show. He cared about his new friends, and he had been eager to perform each night. Of course, he had missed his family, but somehow he'd managed to put them out of his mind most of the time. And then, slowly, the ache for his real home had returned. He saw more clearly that Master Melville acting like he was Sullivan's friend was just that—an act.

It was time for Sullivan and Clarence to move Napoleon behind the stage. An antique cabinet on wheels, it was topped with the upper half of a figure made from wire, cloth, and painted wood.

"Actually," Clarence said as the two of them pushed, "I like hot dogs and beans."

"I don't think that was the point."

Clarence looked around and then spoke quietly. "One thing's for sure, we're definitely moving south. I can tell by how the vegetation has changed. Notice the grass is spiky. And the vines on the tree trunks? It's not as cold during the day, either, although it does get pretty chilly at night."

"I don't understand what we're doing in this old parking lot. There's trash everywhere. I even saw a toilet seat. We could have set up anywhere."

"Could we?" Clarence asked. "When I was getting out the supplies for dinner, I heard Master Melville apologizing to the Black Death for stopping here."

"For once I agree with her."

"But the weird part is how Monty said that we had no choice. He said this spot was on the route and they had to stay on it."

"What route?" Sullivan asked. "It feels to me like we zigzag all over the place."

"I know. But apparently there's a reason."

Sullivan tried to remember what Master Melville had said the other night, when he had opened the back of the caravan. Something about finding what was lost? "Okay," he said, "so we're on a route. But to where exactly? And for what reason? Is it the destination that matters or the places along the way? How was the route decided?"

"Excellent questions," Clarence said. "Too bad I don't have any answers. But there's one thing I do have, and that's the pleasure of watching you juggle eggs on stage tonight. I'm wondering how many you'll break."

"I'm not going to break any."

"We'll see about that." Clarence began to whistle as he walked away.

❊

That night Sullivan watched Frederick's magic act from the wings. Although he had never juggled eggs before, he wasn't too worried. After all, he'd juggled all kinds of fruit—apples, peaches, plums—back when he was starting. He wouldn't try anything fancy but at least he would prove that he could do it.

Sullivan felt a hand on his shoulder and knew immediately that it was Master Melville. "That's it, my boy," he whispered. "Watch Frederick. Let your competitive instinct out. You want to get more applause than a mere magician, don't you? We need a lift, that's for sure, and I'm trusting you to give it to us. I'm sure your new egg routine is going to be a soufflé for the spirit."

Sullivan had no answer for him. These pep talks from Master Melville had begun to make him uneasy. Actually, he *did* feel competitive, only he didn't like to admit it to himself.

"I have to help Clarence get inside Napoleon," he said now, and he walked quickly behind the caravan. Clarence was already there, stripping down to his underwear, which was the only way he could fit in these days. As always, Snit and Snoot sat obediently, staring with dismay as their beloved master disappeared inside the cabinet. Sullivan tipped the upper section back until the latch clicked. He pushed the wheeled contraption around to the side, up the ramp, and onto the stage behind the curtain.

He retreated into the wings and watched. As always, Master Melville opened the cabinet doors to show the audience the wheels and gears inside. He took the key from his pocket and wound the mechanism to bring the automaton to life—or so the audience believed.

Tonight the chess match took longer than usual. Sullivan couldn't tell if Clarence was trying to create suspense or was just having a hard time beating the challenger from the audience. But at last it was checkmate for Napoleon, and as the restless audience applauded with relief, the curtain closed. Sullivan hurried onto the stage and wheeled the automaton off again.

As the dogs jumped eagerly about, Sullivan fumbled for the hidden latch and then tipped the top half over.

"Help me out of here," Clarence wheezed. "I feel like a sardine."

Sullivan took Clarence's sweaty hand and began to pull. "You're definitely . . . too . . . big," he gasped.

At last Clarence popped up with a yelp, throwing

Sullivan backward. The smaller boy took in deep breaths of air. "Man, it feels good to get out of there. Hey, shouldn't you be waiting for your cue?"

"Shoot!" Sullivan sprinted for the stage.

As he arrived he could hear Master Melville stalling in front of the curtain. "You know the old expression, good things take time," he said. "But there's another expression. The show must go on!" He peeked through the curtain and saw Sullivan, a look of both relief and annoyance crossing his face. "And here he is at last, a young man with a mind-boggling talent for keeping things in the air. I give you Dexter, the Accidental Juggler!"

Mistress Melville began to play the "Dill Pickle Rag." She was dressed in black, her beautiful, pale face a contrast to her red lips. The bass drum was strapped to her back, the washboard and cowbells to her front. She had the banjo-ukulele in her hands and around her neck on a wire holder a harmonica, a kazoo, and a whistle. Every so often she rattled the tambourine on her ankle and clanged the cymbal on her shoulder.

Frederick had put out Sullivan's props, including the eggs, which were hidden behind a cardboard cut-out of a chicken, the best idea that he had been able to come up with on short notice. Now Sullivan began his act, pretending to find his set of juggling balls, then tripping and throwing them in the air. The audience laughed and clapped. His confidence grew, as it always did after the initial jitters faded, and he was just turning to pick up the rings when he looked out into the crowd and saw . . .

. . . *Mr. Luria?*

He looked again. It was! It was Mr. Luria, the gym teacher from Beanfield Middle School! Sullivan had gone to Mr. Luria's class on the very day that he had been kidnapped by the medicine show. They had played a game of dodgeball, and Samuel Patinsky had viciously nailed him above the waist but Mr. Luria had refused to call a penalty. Mr. Luria had never liked Sullivan and Sullivan had never liked Mr. Luria, but none of that mattered now. Because there his old teacher was, standing in the second row, a face he actually recognized, someone from his old life who had met his parents and who knew that he had disappeared.

Sullivan began his china pig, toaster, and rubber boot routine. It was technically his hardest, juggling such weirdly shaped objects, but today he hardly concentrated. Why was Mr. Luria so far from Beanfield? Maybe he was taking a weekend holiday (if it was the weekend) or visiting relatives. Sullivan kept performing even as he waited. He waited for Mr. Luria to recognize him. He would think, *Hey, it's that Mintz kid, the one who's missing!* A moment later he would start to shout for someone to call the police. He would jump onto the stage and grab Sullivan. If Master Melville tried to interfere, the muscular Mr. Luria would toss him off the stage like a bale of straw.

Sullivan moved on to the flaming torches. He waited impatiently for Mr. Luria to do something even as he touched a match to the first torch. He used the first to light the other two and began to juggle them, doing a regular cascade, a spin, tossing them under his arms and legs.

Still no sound from his teacher.

And then the truth hit him.

Mr. Luria was not going to call out his name. Mr. Luria was not going to start shouting for the police.

And why? Because Mr. Luria *did not recognize him!* That was how little an impression he had made at school. That was how important he had been in his previous life. Instead, his gym teacher was watching the act with a big, goofy grin on his face. He was enjoying the show just like everyone else.

Sullivan felt so appalled that it was a miracle he didn't drop the flaming torches onto himself. Instead, he doused them and moved towards the cardboard chicken. Even as he was trying to figure out what to do, he bent down and pretended to talk to the cardboard chicken as if it were real. He found one, two, three eggs in the chicken's nest. And when the chicken squawked (actually Mistress Melville blowing into her kazoo), he threw the eggs up into the air.

Sullivan felt more like a zombie than a living person as he performed some basic juggling moves with the eggs. And then it came to him. He would have to call out to Mr. Luria. He would have to tell his old teacher that he was the Beanfield boy who had gone missing. He would throw the eggs one more time, catch them for his finish, and start shouting.

He tossed the eggs high—one, two, three—and took a quick glance down into the crowd.

Mr. Luria was . . . *gone!* Sullivan stared in disbelief.

Splat!

Splat!

Splat!

The first two eggs hit the stage; the last smacked on Sullivan's head. Goo and bits of shell slid down his forehead and into his eyes. The audience remained absolutely silent.

Somebody yanked the curtain. Clarence pulled Sullivan off the stage.

"Well done, omelette head," Frederick said as Sullivan passed him in the wings.

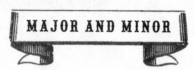

MAJOR AND MINOR

SULLIVAN's humiliation at having dropped all three eggs was nothing compared to his despair at having missed the opportunity to call out to Mr. Luria. He couldn't even bring himself to tell anybody what had happened.

Clarence patted him on the back. "Don't look so glum. Everybody messes up once in a while." And Esmeralda squeezed his arm just before she went on stage. But Sullivan felt wretched as he went behind the caravan and washed the mess off himself with a basin of water and a towel.

All Sullivan wanted to do was crawl into his bunk and feel the wheels moving beneath him as they got away from there. But of course they first had to break down the stage and put away all the gear and snuff out the lanterns and get into their pyjamas.

When all of that was done, Master Melville asked the four performers to gather round. They lined up on the cracked pavement of the parking lot while a full moon shone overhead. "You, too, my dearest," Master Melville said to Mistress, who was picking up her bass drum. "This concerns you the most. You see, I have something for us." He pulled two slips of paper from his vest pocket.

"Don't tell me," Mistress sneered. "We've won the lottery."

"These, my daffodil, are two tickets for the Parsnippity Township Community Theatre production of *The Pirates of Penzance*. I know how you adore Gilbert and Sullivan."

"You mean how *you* adore Gilbert and Sullivan. What row are they?"

"They were very hard to get."

"I asked what row."

"Row Z, on the far aisle."

"I hope you're planning to bring a telescope."

"Such wit, like a fine dry wine. The curtain is in less

than an hour, my dear. We must hurry. Come on, the rest of you, finish up *tout de suite*. Mistress and I have a date!" He shooed them into the caravan.

Sullivan knew well what it meant to have the Melvilles go out for a few hours. It meant that the rest of them would get to hold an old-life party. At an old-life party, they talked about their lives back home, sharing memories of birthday parties, or funny incidents with their parents or siblings or friends. They remembered times when they were happy or sad. They made decorations and put together snacks, and Frederick always concocted his famous punch. They listened to music. These nights always had something magical about them and never failed to lift Sullivan's spirits. Master Melville never admitted that he knew about the old-life parties, but he would help them to get ready by leaving out food and other things they needed.

But this time was different. Master Melville usually gave them a full day to prepare, and here they were already being shut up for the night. They didn't have anything ready.

"It isn't fair," Clarence hissed as soon as the door was shut behind them, blocking out the moonlight. "We haven't had an old-life party in ages and he pulls this on us?"

"We might as well just go to sleep," Frederick said, flapping his blanket straight.

It really was the worst luck. Sullivan needed an old-life party to cheer him up. He heard the door open again and looked up to see Master Melville peering in.

"Sorry, chaps. Couldn't be helped. It was very last minute. Here, this is the best I can do."

He left something on the floor. Then he closed the door and locked it. Another few moments and then hooves sounded on the concrete as the Melvilles trotted away on Soggy Biscuit.

"We might as well see what Monty left us," Clarence said. "I've still got a stub of candle left over. Hold on a sec."

He fumbled around. A match flared, and then the more steady light of the candle. Frederick leaned down from his bunk to look. "Jujubes," Clarence said. "Somebody in the crowd must have dropped them."

"Is it a full package, at least?" Frederick asked.

"Not even half. Let me count. There's eight of them, two each. We might as well stretch out the enjoyment. Everybody just take one for now."

They sat on their bunks. Clarence came to each in turn, holding out the open package. Sullivan was last.

"No, that's okay," he said. "Somebody else can eat mine."

"Sorry, not allowed," Esmeralda insisted.

"Okay. I'll take the yellow one."

"To match the yellow that landed on your head tonight?" Frederick said.

"That's low," Clarence muttered.

"It was a joke."

"Then you have the worst sense of humour."

"It doesn't matter," Sullivan said. He held the jujube in his hand.

"What *is* the matter?" Esmeralda asked, coming to sit beside him on his bunk. "It can't just be your performance. Something else is going on."

Sullivan looked away. "I can't bear to say it."

"We're your friends," Clarence said. "Even Frederick, although he doesn't show it."

"That's nasty," Frederick said. "I just don't need everybody to think I'm adorable, like you do. Go ahead, Dexter."

"All right, I'll tell you. I saw somebody I knew in the audience tonight."

"Who was it?" Clarence asked.

"The gym teacher from my school."

"He must have recognized you."

"Well, he didn't. Shows how memorable I was."

"What did you do?" asked Frederick. Even he leaned forward in his bunk to hear.

"I didn't do anything. I didn't shout or make a face or jump off the stage. I mean, I was going to, but I waited too long and then he was gone. And you know why I waited so long? Because there's something the matter with me. Because I like being a prisoner, separated from my family. And I'm sure there's nothing you can say to make me feel better."

Silence. The candle wavered a moment and became still again. Their faces were a yellowish-red in the light, while the corners of the caravan faded into darkness.

"I'll tell you why," Clarence said. "Because something has happened to us. *Inside* us. There are chains keeping us here that we can't see. They're invisible."

"That's the very worst thing I've ever heard," Esmeralda said.

"Yes," Clarence agreed. "Yes, it is."

Sullivan put the jujube into his mouth and started to chew. Clarence's words touched something inside him, some deep thought or truth that he could feel but didn't have words for. "You're right," he said, the jujube sticking to his teeth. "But I think there's something more than that. Something else that's also keeping us here. It isn't just that we don't think we can leave."

Frederick said, "Yes. It's also because we don't want to leave. Not just me. All of us."

The words shocked Sullivan. They shocked him

because in his mind he tried to disagree but couldn't. "What exactly do you mean?" he asked.

Frederick flicked his hair out of his eyes. "All right, I'll tell you, but you have to actually listen to me. First of all, you need to understand that there are the major arts and the minor arts."

"A lecture!" Clarence exclaimed. "Should we take notes?"

"If you don't want to hear it, that's fine with me. I'll save my breath."

"No," Esmeralda said. "Go ahead."

"All right. As I said, there are the major and the minor arts. The major arts are the kind everybody knows—the symphony, the opera, ballet, theatre. But then there are the minor arts. That's the category that we fall into. Conjuring. Juggling. Tightrope walking. All except dog training. That's even lower, somewhere down with making balloon animals and doing yo-yo tricks."

"Very funny," Clarence grumbled. "And you whistle through your nose when you sleep. Is that a minor art, too?"

"Let me get this straight," Sullivan said. "You're basically saying that we're doomed to always be in the minor leagues."

"Not exactly." Frederick's voice grew more

confident. "Here's the important thing. It's possible for a minor art to rise to the level of a major art."

"Huh?" Clarence shook his head. "Can you run that by me again?"

"Listen carefully. First, you need to take your skills to an extremely high level. And then you need to use those skills to serve a greater purpose—to create a drama that will not just entertain people but will move them."

"In their minds *and* their hearts," Esmeralda said.

"Exactly. That's when your little bag of tricks turns into something great."

"And I bet I know what you're going to say next." Clarence leaned back in his bunk. "That you're the only one who's managed to do it."

"You really think I'm that arrogant? Of course I haven't done it. When Charlie Chaplin did his comic routines back in the days of silent pictures, he made people laugh and he made them cry at the same time. When Houdini performed his escape act, he made people face their own fear of death. *They* were great artists. I'm not even close. But the difference between me and the rest of you is that I want to be great. I have that ambition. And in my opinion, anyone who doesn't is just a hack."

"Freddy," Esmeralda gently admonished, "that's putting it a bit strong."

"It's what I think. And actually, I don't really think I'm different from the rest of you. Except for the fact that I've admitted the truth to myself. I want to be a great performer. *That's* what's holding me here. I get a chance to perform every night, to become better. I think that's what's holding the rest of you, too. You just don't want to admit it."

Once more they fell into silence. Sullivan closed his eyes. He knew that Frederick was right. He *did* want to be a great artist. If he went back home now, back to school and chores and regular life, he'd never get the chance. Maybe that was the reason he hadn't called out to Mr. Luria. He wasn't ready.

Clarence broke the silence. "This sure is some old-life party. We haven't even used our real names. Maybe we've become too attached to the new ones."

"Okay, I've had enough of this gloomy soul-searching," Esmeralda announced. "I don't know about you but I want some music."

"Only we don't have anything to make music with."

"Come on, you can make music anywhere. Let me see." Esmeralda searched around her bunk. "This might do," she said, coming up with a Smarties box. Sullivan knew she used it to hold the safety pins for attaching ribbons to her costume. She began to shake it, *cha-cha, cha-cha.*

"Not bad," Clarence said. He too looked about, and from under his bed he came up with the cookie tin that he kept dog treats in. Immediately Snit and Snoot sat up and held out their paws. Clarence opened the tin, tossed each dog a treat, and closed it again. Then he put the tin in his lap and began drumming on it to match Esmeralda's rhythm.

"This is like kindergarten," Frederick said. "Aw well, I might as well get in on it." He hunted under his own bunk and came up with the fishing tackle box where he kept the things he needed to repair his magic effects. He found three long rubber bands and stretched them around the open box. Plucked, they made a dull twang.

Sullivan didn't feel like being part of any music-making. The effects of the day—of seeing Mr. Luria, and dropping the eggs, and listening to Frederick say they really didn't want to leave—had all been too much. But he didn't like to spoil things either, so he felt under his own bunk to pull out his box of juggling gear. Inside was the china pig wrapped in an old shirt. The pig had a slot in its mouth for putting in money and a bigger hole in its belly for taking the money out. Sullivan held up the pig and put his lips to the snout while covering the belly with his palm. When he blew, a long, airy note came out.

"All right!" cried Clarence. "Play that thing!"

So Sullivan began to blow, short notes and longer ones, keeping to the jumpy rhythm as he raised the pig up like a trumpet. And then Esmeralda stood up and began dancing and Clarence got up to join her, still banging his drum. It all sounded and looked ridiculous, Sullivan thought, but it eased his heart a little.

* 5 *

COPYCAT

$\mathcal{T}$O young Jinny Mintz, the town of Tinzler did not look promising. The movie theatre had been turned into a flea market selling old clothes and broken lamps. The diner and the barber shop were closed up. At least the ice cream parlour was open, but the only flavour it served was lingonberry. Jinny had never even *heard* of lingonberry before.

"This town certainly looks as if it has fallen on hard times," Manny observed.

"Just like us," Jinny said.

They sat on a wooden bench on Main Street while

Jinny licked her ice cream. Just yesterday they had seemed to be getting somewhere. In the previous town they had met a ten-year-old boy who'd told them that a kid on his baseball team had heard from a girl at the park about some kind of show that had taken place outside of Tinzler last Friday. And here they were, after a six-hour bus ride, and not a single person they had spoken to knew about any show.

"The trail has grown cold," Manny intoned.

"Colder than this ice cream, which is all mooshy. Can we go to the library?"

"I don't expect this town has a library."

"Then how come it says *Public Library* on that sign beside the barber shop? And it's open Tuesdays, which is today. And it also says *Everyone Welcome.*"

Manny looked across the road and squinted to see the sign more clearly. "You read that by yourself?"

"Sure. I can read lots more than that."

"Why didn't you tell me?"

"You didn't ask."

She let Manny finish the end of her ice cream and then they crossed the empty street. The sign had an arrow pointing up, so they went through the door beside the barber shop and up to the second floor. Jinny hopped up the steps two at a time while Manny followed, carefully holding the rail.

The library was a single long room lined with shelves, with more books displayed on tables. A woman sat at a desk, stamping a pile of books.

"Good afternoon," Manny said.

"And to you," the woman smiled. "I don't believe you're from around here. I know all the regular users."

"We're just passing through. Mind if we look around?"

"Please do. Perhaps the young lady would like to know where the picture books are."

"Yes, please. I would also like to know why boring grown-up books don't have any pictures."

"That's a good question," the librarian said. "Do you have any favourites?"

"I like the book about the mouse who's a dentist. And I like Dr. Seuss. He's deep."

A few moments later Jinny was sitting on a pillow with a stack of books beside her while Manny browsed among the hardcovers displayed on the tables. He saw a community bulletin board on the wall and began to examine the notices: a hockey-league schedule, rules for recycling, an advertisement by somebody who painted portraits of dogs. On the left side was a hand-lettered title, *One Hundred Years Ago Today*, and underneath was pinned the front page of the local Tinzler newspaper. Manny read the headlines: *Mayor*

Brings Goat to Council Meeting. Spectacle Factory Holds Employee Picnic.

"I see you've noticed our local history display," the librarian said. "I just started putting those up a month ago. I think it's fascinating to know what was going on back then. Tinzler used to be a bigger town. We had a factory that made eyeglasses. On the side of the factory building was a big sign that said *Wear Tinzler Spectacles and See the View.*"

"Yes, it's very interesting," Manny said politely, rubbing his goatee. "I suppose there used to be a lot of travelling medicine shows back then."

"Yes, there were. In fact, there was a mention of one in the newspaper that I had up last week."

Manny turned around. "Pardon me?"

"There was an article in the newspaper about a medicine show."

"May I see it?"

"Of course. I'll just get it out of the archives."

Manny watched the librarian move to a metal filing cabinet at the end of the room. She opened it and searched through the hanging files. Then she pulled out a newspaper protected by a clear plastic sleeve. She carried it over and laid it on the table. Manny leaned down to see better. A headline read: *Medicine Show Attracts Big Crowd.*

"Jinny, you'd better come see this."

"But I'm reading about a dog who farts."

"A very popular book," said the librarian.

"Yes, I'm sure," Manny said impatiently. "But this is really a very odd coincidence, Jinny."

"Okay, okay, hold your hamsters, I'm coming."

Jinny got up with a huff and came over to stand beside Manny. Manny began to read aloud.

Our town has seen many fine performers grace the stage of the Tinzler Theatre. But this past Friday an entertainment of a different order set up its modest stage behind the eyeglass factory in order to attract the attention of the workers.

While other medicine shows have put up here before, this one was notable as all its performers were children—all except for a chess-playing automaton. The proprietors of the show are a husband-and-wife team by the name of Melville. While the female half produced the musical effects, the husband acted as master of ceremonies.

It is the opinion of this newspaper that many of these medicine pitchmen are no better than thieves and charlatans. However, Master Melville claims that his Hop-Hop Drops are a unique combination of ingredients, prepared with great difficulty, and are guaranteed to bring general happiness. In fact, he is so confident that he is offering a reward to anyone who can prove they do not work.

Manny leaned away from the bulletin board. "Do you see, Jinny? This medicine show had children in it too."

Jinny began jumping up and down. "I remember now. That's his name! That's his name! *Melville.*"

"Whose name?"

"The man who talked and danced and held up the little bottle. His name was Master Melville."

"But Jinny, this article is about a show that came here a hundred years ago. These people must all be dead by now."

"I don't care. That's still his name. And those are the drops he sold. Hop-Hop Drops."

"I think I had better sit down," Manny said.

Seeing his distress, the librarian pulled over a chair.

"Thank you," Manny said. "Jinny, I know you're an unusually smart and observant girl, so let me ask you one last time. Tell me if you have even a little bit of doubt."

"I'm four hundred percent sure. And a half."

"This is very, very strange. A medicine show existed

a hundred years ago with the same name? How can that be?"

Jinny scrunched up her face. "Manny, did my brother go backward in time? Is that where he is, a hundred years ago?"

"No, I believe we can rule that out. But that's about all I'm sure of. Miss, can we make a few copies of this?"

"How exciting," said the librarian. "I love a good mystery. Copies are ten cents a page."

"This is a clue, Jinny, the best clue we've had so far. We just have to figure out what it means. I think we should look at that factory site. Maybe we'll find something there."

"Oh, the factory was torn down twenty years ago," the librarian said. "There's an old used-car dealership there now. And it's closed, too."

❊

When Manny and Jinny got to the car dealership, all they found was a low, empty building with faded signs in the window, and a square parking lot littered with paper cups and other garbage. They walked slowly about, looking at the ground for signs that Sullivan and the medicine show had been there. Jinny found a pink ribbon and Manny found a playing card. Off to the side, where the weedy grass began, they came across a firepit that looked as if it had been used recently.

"None of this is proof," Manny said, "but it does look as if the show might have been here. It's a strange feeling, isn't it, the possibility that Sullivan was standing right where we are now?"

Manny watched Jinny close her eyes and smile. She put her arms out, as if she were hugging an invisible person. Then she opened her eyes again. "Can we stay here tonight?" she asked.

"I don't see why not. There's no hotel in town anyway."

The pair moved a short distance to be near a stand of scrawny sycamore trees. Now that the other parents were helping to support them, they were much better outfitted for travel. They had an ultralight and fully waterproof tent and two warm sleeping bags that rolled up very small. Manny could never figure out how to put up the tent, with its flexible, high-tech rods that snapped together, but Jinny could do it in three minutes flat. Soon they had a fire going in the pit. They waited for the flames to settle and the water to boil before making macaroni and cheese in a tin pot. Jinny sat cross-legged on the ground and Manny perched on an overturned paint can, and they held their plates in their laps.

"I keep thinking," Manny said as he forked up some macaroni. "Some couple is travelling around with a bunch of kidnapped kids and putting on a show that has the same name as another show from a hundred years ago. What could it mean?"

"I'll tell you what it means," Jinny said even as she ate. "It means that the man and the woman are copycats."

"Why, you're absolutely right! For some reason I didn't connect the dots. This new show must be deliberately imitating the old one."

"So do we understand now?"

"Not exactly. We know what they're doing but we don't know why. There is one thing more that I've just realized. If the new show was here last Friday, that means they performed at the same place and on the same date as the old one, exactly one hundred years later. Which means that the new show must be following the exact schedule as the old one. If we could find out the old medicine show's route, then we would know where the new show is going. We could get there first."

"And find Sullivan?"

"That's the idea. The only problem is, we don't know the route of the old show. But maybe we can find it out. Maybe there are other articles in other old newspapers. Your mother is good at researching. She's always looking things up for her poems. I bet she can help. This is good, Jinny. This is very good."

The two friends sat by the fire for a while longer. The scrawny trees didn't hide the parking lot beside them. They crawled into the tent and slipped into their warm sleeping bags. Jinny did feel strange, knowing that just last week her dear brother had been at this very same spot. She tried to feel his presence, as if he were still there, but it was hard. She hadn't seen him for so long, months and months. Did he look the same? Did he sound the same? Had he changed so much because of all the things that had happened to him that he wouldn't be her brother any more?

"Good night, Jinny," Manny said.

Jinny sighed. "Are you going to snore again tonight?"

"I can't say for sure."

"I don't mind. You sound like a bear. A nice bear."

"You make noises too. Little, bitty noises. *Pip-pip-pip.*"

"I do?"

"Like a little bird."

"Ha! We're a bird and a bear."

"*Snore, snore, snore.*"

"*Pip-pip-pip.*"

Then they were quiet. Jinny said a silent good night to Sullivan, and to her parents, just as she did every night, and then she fell asleep.

THE ACCIDENT

OST days in a person's life are destined to blur in memory with all the days before and after. But a day that is destined to be remembered, both for what happens during it and what happens after—such a day begins in exactly the same way. It looks perfectly ordinary.

It was a peculiar fact that, for Sullivan, an ordinary day meant waking up without having the slightest idea where he was. But he was used to emerging into a landscape different from the one he had seen the night before. This morning he found the caravan stopped

· 57 ·

right next to a steep riverbank beside an old grain mill. The mill had long ago fallen into disuse, but the giant millstone was still inside the wooden structure, built over a fast-moving water.

Mistress Melville was having one of her unwell spells and did not come out. Frederick volunteered to brew her a pot of herbal tea. None of the performers was ever allowed inside the Melvilles' side of the caravan, so he left the tea and a couple of biscuits beside the small door behind the caravan driver's seat.

After breakfast it was Clarence and Sullivan's turn to clean up.

"What's with Frederick?" Clarence asked, dumping dirty dishes into the basin of hot water.

"What do you mean?"

"The way he's sucking up to the Black Death. I mean, he's always been this way, but lately he's gotten worse. It's like she's cast a spell on him or something. When she needs something, he jumps." Clarence shook his head.

Actually, Sullivan had noticed it too. He wondered if it had anything to do with Frederick's home life before the medicine show. All Sullivan knew was that Frederick had been an orphan and had been raised by an uncle who had made him work. But if what Freddy needed was some motherly affection, he wasn't likely to get it from the Black Death.

"Anyway, Clarence, I don't think you should tease him about it," said Sullivan.

"Tease him? *Moi?*"

"Yes, you. And now I've got equestrian duty."

Sullivan's other task this morning was to look after Soggy Biscuit. Nobody knew exactly how old Soggy was, not even Master Melville. Everyone liked taking care of the horse, although it was generally agreed that Esmeralda had a special relationship with him. Sullivan sometimes thought that having the horse around was like a kind of therapy for the performers. Everyone whispered secrets to Soggy; everyone gave him treats and stroked his nose and even kissed him. He was a comfort to them all.

First, Sullivan worked on Soggy's hooves. He only had to run his hand along the back of Soggy's lower leg and say "Up!" for him to raise his foot. Sullivan used a hoof pick to scrape out any stones and dirt. He did one foot after another, patting Soggy and reassuring him. Next he used a brush, working over the horse's coat.

Sullivan heard a whistle. Soggy whinnied with pleasure, recognizing it as Esmeralda's. She came up beside them and said, "I hope you're doing a good job on my buddy."

"Don't worry, I am."

The horse nudged Esmeralda and she scratched him between his pointed ears. "You're a good horse, aren't you?" she cooed. She said to Sullivan, "I worry about Soggy. The Melvilles work him so hard every night. What is going to happen when he's not up to it?"

"Oh, Soggy will be all right." But he thought to himself that Esmeralda had just given him something else to worry about. Only he didn't want to think about that now. He wanted to find his courage and somehow get closer to Essy. He'd had feelings for her almost from the first day of arriving at the medicine show. If only he had some way of knowing how *she* felt. He took a deep breath and—

"Dex?"

"Yes, Essy?"

"I want to talk to you about something."

"You do?"

"Yes. About Frederick."

Sullivan's hopes sank again. "Sure."

"I don't think people are being very nice to him . . ."

As she talked on, Sullivan looked over to the river. He noticed a figure moving inside the old mill building; some missing planks let him see inside. It was Master Melville. He was lifting something to peer underneath it. This wasn't the first time that Sullivan had seen Master Melville searching, poking about in dense shrubs, looking under old barrels or piles of rocks.

"Are you even listening to me, Dexter?"

"Of course I am. And I'll try to be nicer to Frederick."

"Thanks, Dex. I know this is a weird thing to say, but I'm glad you're here. Not for your sake but for mine."

She put her hand on his arm a moment and then she walked away. He watched her dreamily, until Soggy Biscuit nudged the back of his head, wanting to be petted.

❖

That evening, Master Melville changed the program order around. He thought it made them perform better. As Sullivan waited in the wings for his cue from Master Melville, he thought about what Frederick had said at the old-life party. When Sullivan had first started juggling, his only goal had been to keep three or four balls in the air without dropping them. Just doing that had been enough. Then, when he'd begun to perform in the medicine show, he had just wanted to keep people entertained. He could do that now, and more than that. He made people laugh with pleasure and gasp with amazement. But now it didn't seem like enough. Had he always wanted to be an artist without realizing it?

"I present to you . . . Dexter, the Accidental Juggler!"

Polite applause greeted Sullivan as he stepped onto the stage. Maybe he couldn't be a great artist tonight but at least he could be a good juggler. He cleared every other thought from his mind and focused on the here and now. His movements were sure, his throws exact, and his catches crisp. Even his acting was better than usual, and the audience reacted with more laughter and applause.

When he came off stage again, Master Melville patted him on the shoulder. "Well done, my boy, well done! Now, *that's* juggling. You are an example to the others."

Sullivan couldn't help enjoying the compliment. He went to the caravan to help Clarence get into Napoleon.

"What got into you tonight?" Clarence asked as he began to strip down. "You were smokin'. You think some Hollywood agent is out there? You think the next big thing is going to be a *juggling* movie?"

"No, the next big thing will be a movie about a kid who plays chess in his underwear. You'd better hurry up."

Sullivan unlatched Napoleon and opened the top. Clarence put in one foot while grabbing onto his friend's arm. "I hate how tight it is in here. But try telling that to the Black Death. She thinks I'm growing on purpose. 'Ah, that boy. He eats too much!'"

Sullivan closed the top and wheeled Napoleon around to the wings, where Frederick helped him push it up onto the stage behind the curtain. Master Melville finished his introduction and Esmeralda pulled open the curtain. Sullivan became lost in his own thoughts until he heard Master Melville say, "Napoleon's in a tight situation. I don't know if the old mess of gears and wheels will get out of this one." Apparently, Clarence was having trouble winning the game. Another move and the man had Napoleon in check with his queen and rook.

Sullivan saw Napoleon raise an arm and then close its wooden fingers on a bishop. It raised the piece into the air but then the arm stopped.

"Very interesting." There was a note of unease in Master Melville's voice. "It appears that Napoleon is thinking twice about his move." What was Clarence doing, exactly—trying to create more suspense?

Napoleon's wooden fingers opened and the bishop fell to the board, knocking several pieces over.

"How clumsy of you, Napoleon." Master Melville

pretended to laugh. "I'm sure the automaton will pick the bishop up again. Won't you, Napoleon?"

Another pause and then the wooden arm came down heavily, flinging wooden chess pieces everywhere. The arm rested on the chessboard and didn't move.

"Quick!" hissed Master Melville. "Close the curtain!"

Something was very wrong. Sullivan scrambled onto the stage, Esmeralda hurried from the other side, and Frederick began to yank the curtain shut. "There's no time to move it!" Esmeralda said. "We have to get him out now."

Sullivan fumbled for the hidden latch. Panic made his hands clumsy, but at last he found it and pulled over the top half of the automaton.

On the other side of the curtain, Master Melville was telling the crowd that the show was over. Sullivan could see the back of Clarence's sweaty head, but his face was tilted downward. Esmeralda shrieked as the two of them grabbed hold of Clarence under his arms and began to pull. His body felt clammy. They pushed and yanked and finally extracted him from the cabinet and laid him down on the stage.

"He's blue!" Esmeralda cried.

"I don't think he's breathing. I've got to remember how to do CPR."

The dogs appeared and began to whine. From out front came the sound of Mistress playing music. Sullivan tried to remember his school first-aid lessons. Did he tilt the head back? Did he pinch the nose?

"Move over." Esmeralda pushed him aside. She put her mouth over Clarence's and exhaled into his lungs. She turned her head to see his chest rise and fall, then did it again.

"Is he all right?" Frederick asked, coming over and kneeling down. "He's dead, isn't he? It's horrible . . ."

Esmeralda continued—a breath in, a pause, another. Now Master Melville came from around the curtain. An awful feeling descended on Sullivan, as if the world were growing smaller and smaller.

Clarence coughed. His body began shaking. Esmeralda leaned away and Clarence coughed some more, then took in several gasping breaths. His skin turned white and then pink again.

"He's alive!"

Clarence began to breathe more regularly, blinking and looking about as if he had just woken up.

"Can you hear me?" Frederick asked.

Clarence tried to speak. "My mom makes . . . very good . . . apple . . . pie."

"I'm sure she does!" Esmeralda laughed, tears in her eyes. "But don't talk. You need to take it easy."

Clarence looked down at himself. "I . . . I seem to have . . . lost my clothes."

Master Melville sent the last audience stragglers away. Then Sullivan and the others began to take down the stage. Each of them went over to check on Clarence, who lay back against a tree, recovering his strength.

"You can't ever go back in that thing," Esmeralda said as she threw out the basin of water. "You scared us sick."

"I don't think I *can* go back in. I don't fit any more."

"Ah, you were just trying to get some attention," Frederick said.

"What a thing to say!" Sullivan jumped in.

"Why does nobody ever know when I'm joking?"

"*I* knew it," Clarence wheezed.

As they stood in the dark, Sullivan heard Mistress's voice coming from the other side of the caravan. At first he couldn't hear what she was saying, only that she was angry. But then her voice grew louder—loud enough for everyone to notice.

"Useless boy! And what will we do now that we're an act short? You think we'll sell as many bottles? Of course we won't."

Sullivan looked at Clarence, who smiled with embarrassment. Master Melville spoke next, but his voice was harder to hear. He was clearly trying to placate Mistress, but she wasn't having any of it.

"You're not only soft-hearted, you're also soft-headed. What have we got for all our troubles? Absolutely nothing. And why are these dogs pestering me? Get away, revolting animals."

The dogs usually kept close to Clarence, but Sullivan couldn't see them anywhere. Clarence, too, looked about. They must have wandered to the other side of the caravan. Snit and Snoot never liked hearing angry voices. They would jump up on people to try to make them stop.

"Damn these tick-infested mongrels! Get away from me, get away, I say!"

A loud squeal. A thud. One of the dogs began to bark and growl.

"What have you done?" cried Master Melville.

"Me? I hardly did a thing. I'm sure it's faking. Just wake it up."

"Come on, doggy, wake up now. Move your tail or something. This is bad, Eudora, very bad!"

Sullivan saw Clarence's eyes go wide. He struggled up from the ground and, although he was still weak, dragged himself towards the voices. Sullivan went after, with Esmeralda and Frederick following.

On the other side of the caravan, Master and

Mistress Melville were looking down over the edge of the riverbank. Snoot was pawing at the edge, whining and barking, trying to get down. Sullivan and Frederick helped Clarence over to the edge where they all stared down in horror. Eight or nine feet below, a line of jagged rocks lay half-buried in the sandy shore. Between two of them lay Snit.

"Snit!"

"Clarence, don't!" Esmeralda called. But it was too late. Clarence was already sliding down the bank. All Sullivan and Frederick managed to do was grab his arms and lower him down to the bottom. Clarence knelt beside Snit and put the dog's head in his lap.

"Snit! What is it, boy, what's wrong? You're all right, you have to be. Please move, Snit." But the dog didn't move.

Sullivan ran along the riverbank until he came to a place that wasn't as steep and worked his way down. He ran along the edge of the water until he reached them. He slipped between the rocks and kneeled down. Snit's eyes were closed

"I think he must have broken his neck," Clarence said.

"I don't understand," Mistress said from the bank above. "All I did was push him away from me. He must have been very clumsy to fall backward like that."

"I'm very sorry," Master Melville said quietly. "It was an accident."

Sullivan saw Clarence put his cheek against the body of his dog. "Snit, oh, Snit." He began to cry quietly. "What am I going to do without you?"

"This is unbearable," Esmeralda said. "We have to help him somehow."

"We can carry Snit up," Frederick said. He began to walk along the bank with Esmeralda. Sullivan waited for them to get down and he and Frederick carried the dog, although it hardly took two people. Esmeralda held on to Clarence's arm. "We'll find a nice spot to bury him," she said gently. "A pretty spot near the water. Snit always liked playing in the water."

❄

In the dark, Sullivan, Frederick, and Esmeralda took turns with the spade. They dug the grave under a willow tree. Master Melville watched from a distance, but Mistress did not come out of the caravan.

"He was a wonderful dog," Sullivan said. "A good and loyal friend to Clarence. He had a joyful heart and he made all our days better."

Clarence tried to speak, but he was unable to get any words out. Snoot whimpered, and Clarence leaned down and let her lick his face. He picked up the spade and threw a couple of shovels of earth into the grave but was too weak to do more. He let the others finish.

At last Master Melville came towards them. "It's very late. We must be on our way."

Clarence didn't protest. He got up and, making sure that Snoot stayed with him, headed for the caravan. Sullivan and the others followed.

"A sad day," Master Melville said.

One after another they climbed into the back of the caravan and got into their bunks. They changed under the covers into their pyjamas. The door closed, the lock clicked. The caravan started to move.

THE HARD ROAD

Master Melville's Medicine Show

ON they travelled.

They performed by a marsh where long-legged birds walked daintily through the shallows and tiny frogs chirped incessantly.

They performed beside an old stone quarry, their voices echoing back to them.

They performed by a car graveyard, hundreds of old, rusting hulks piled one on top of another.

One night Frederick found a snake in his bed.

One night Esmeralda stood up while asleep and began to walk an imaginary tightrope.

One night Sullivan woke with a fever. He fell into a delirious state, muttered names and half sentences, tried to crawl out of bed. Two days later, when the fever finally broke, he looked up to see Esmeralda cooling his forehead with a damp cloth.

One afternoon it rained hard, heavy sheets of water smacking the caravan, the sky cracked by lightning streaks. They stayed inside and played gin rummy with Frederick's cards.

One night the caravan jolted them awake. A wheel had broken. They had to lift the end of the caravan while Master Melville fixed it.

One evening they played to a group of rowdy men who drank from bottles in paper bags and shouted insults.

One evening they played to just seven people who told them that everybody was watching a baseball game on television.

One evening Frederick sneezed and dropped the coins hidden between his fingers.

One evening Master Melville slipped on the stage and pulled down the curtain.

One evening Sullivan nearly set his hair on fire.

One evening, one morning, one night, one after-noon . . .

❊

Clarence kept Snoot close by him. Both the boy and the dog mourned the loss of their companion. Sullivan spent more time with Clarence, mostly just sitting without talking, sometimes scratching Snoot on her belly. Even Frederick was careful around Clarence. And Sullivan could see that Master Melville was watching too, judging how little he ate, noticing how listlessly he stood about, neither performing nor helping nor even complaining. As for Mistress, she avoided him. If she saw Clarence walking in her direction, she would turn away. Even the Black Death, Sullivan realized, could feel guilt and remorse.

Putting on the show without the dog act as well as Napoleon was a trial for the remaining three performers. They each had to stretch their acts another ten minutes, adding routines that weren't ready and padding the old ones. Sometimes people drifted away from the show, something that had never happened before. Any hope that Sullivan had of reaching a higher level of artistry became a wistful dream.

And yet the show carried on, moving from one site to another. Sullivan noticed that Master Melville spent even more of each day walking about, lifting old boards, peering down holes, digging around fence posts.

One evening at dinner Clarence surprised them all by announcing that he would soon rejoin the show. He had been thinking long and hard and had come up with ways to modify the act so that he could perform with Snoot alone.

"Delighted. Absolutely delighted, my boy." Master Melville patted him on the back.

And the next day, Clarence began to practise. He used all the tricks that Snoot already knew—standing on her hind legs, jumping, rolling over, walking on a barrel. And when they performed on stage together for the first time, the audience applauded. It wasn't as good as the old act, but it worked.

After the show, Sullivan and Clarence took down the stage together. Sullivan said, "I think it's good that you're performing again. It takes a lot of strength, Clarence."

"I'm not doing it for me. And I'm certainly not doing it for *them*. But I know you and the others were carrying too much. And I did it for Snoot, too. She was depressed. I think she's even more heartbroken than I am. I couldn't just let her mope around and do nothing."

HOW TO PLAY BOINGA

MANNY Morgenstern used the post office in Tinzler to send copies of the newspaper article to the families of the four missing children. ("Why didn't you just scan it and send it by e-mail?" asked Ellen Raskin, mother of the red-haired girl, over the telephone. "Because I don't know what a scan is," Manny replied.) The discovery caused a flurry of excited phone calls for several days.

But when people read the article for the third and fourth time, their excitement turned to confusion. What exactly did this new information mean?

A medicine show with the same name had existed a hundred years ago? How would that help them find their kids? Did Manny's insistence that the new medicine show was following the exact route and schedule as the old one really make sense? And since they didn't have the route or the schedule, what use was the knowledge anyway?

One person who refused to be disappointed was Loretta Mintz. "This is the first real clue we've had in ages," she told her husband, Gilbert. "I'm not going to throw up my hands and say we can't learn something from it." She had begun going to the Beanfield library to use the computer and search online newspaper archives. She'd looked at newspapers dated after the one Manny found, searching their headlines page after page. So far she hadn't found anything, but she wasn't discouraged yet.

And in the meantime, she told Gilbert one evening, they still had the newspaper that Manny found to read for clues. It was late, and the residents of the Stardust Home for Old People had retired to their rooms. Most of them didn't sleep very well (old people rarely do), and every so often Gilbert or Loretta would check to make sure that nobody had become lost wandering the halls, or was in the kitchen trying to make a cup of tea and possibly burning the place down.

"The thing is," Gilbert said, "I've read that old article a dozen times and I still don't know what to make of it."

"Then let's put our heads together and think," Loretta suggested. "So, what exactly *do* we know? We know that something called Master Melville's Medicine Show toured the country a hundred years ago."

"Right," said Gilbert. "And we know that it was run by a husband and wife. He was the master of ceremonies. She made the music. All the performers were children."

"Except that automaton," Loretta corrected. "Apparently that was some sort of machine."

"They sold medicine in a bottle," Gilbert said. "Hop-Hop Drops. It had a secret recipe. The Melvilles were planning to offer a reward to anyone who could prove it didn't work."

"So there are several mysteries here. Who were the Melvilles? Where did the children come from? What sort of reward were they offering? And, of course, where was the medicine show going next?"

"Questions without answers," Gilbert said. "But at least they're precise questions."

"And that's just the original show," Loretta continued. What about the new, copycat show, to use Jinny's term? Let's assume they really are trying to duplicate the original show. How would these people go about doing that?"

"For one thing, they'd have to adopt the names of the original couple, Montague and Eudora Melville. Not very common names these days. They would also have to build a caravan. Jinny says it looks just like the picture in the old newspaper. So they must have seen a picture of it too. And then there are the Hop-Hop Drops, which I suppose they have to make."

"That would mean these people have the secret recipe," Loretta mused.

"Yes, if they're making the stuff the same way."

"Maybe the drops really are amazing," Loretta said, "and this couple is trying to make a fortune selling them."

"Is that likely? If the drops really work, why not sell the recipe to some big company that manufactures medicine? Why not sell it in drug stores and shopping malls instead of out of the back of a caravan?" Gilbert reasoned.

"Okay, you're right. Maybe it's time to call the police again. The ones who tried to help when Sullivan disappeared."

"Officers Spoonitch and Forka? That's a good idea. I'll have to try not to laugh this time when I say their names."

"Gilbert, that's rude!"

"I know it is," he said, already starting to chuckle.

"At least you still can laugh," Loretta said, unable to join in.

❉

Gilbert telephoned the police station and asked to speak to Officer Spoonitch or Officer Forka. He was surprised to hear the desk sergeant laugh. Then the sergeant said something with the phone muffled, and other voices laughed, too. There was even more background noise after that, but finally Officer Spoonitch got on the phone.

"Is something going on there?" Gilbert asked.

"Sorry about that," Officer Spoonitch said. "A little celebration, that's all. Now, how can I help you, Mr. Mintz? As you know, your son's case is closed."

"Yes, but we've got new information."

"New information, you say? The timing is rather bad. You see, I'm about to go on vacation."

"I really think you should see it."

"Hang on a moment."

Officer Spoonitch consulted with somebody else. There was more laughter in the background and then the sound of cheering. At last the officer got back on the phone.

"Officer Forka and I can come right now. I'm afraid we can't stay long."

❄

Loretta and Gilbert waited for the officers by the front door of the Stardust Home. They could see a few snowflakes floating gently down, the first of winter. Both of them had the same silent thought: Was Sullivan warm enough? Behind them, in one of the sitting rooms, a dozen residents sat in armchairs or stood with their walkers, waiting too. Gilbert had the copy of the old newspaper article in his hand. At last the police car pulled up to the curb.

"Here they come," Loretta announced. "Are those tin cans tied to their car?"

Officer Forka got out first. She was wearing a long white gown with puffy sleeves.

"Is that a wedding dress?" Gilbert asked.

Officer Spoonitch got out next. He was wearing a tuxedo. Gilbert opened the door as they came up. There was confetti in the officers' hair.

"You got married!" said Loretta.

"We're together so much we decided that we might as well," said Officer Spoonitch.

"I hope that wasn't the reason!" Officer Forka playfully pushed her new husband. "Now my name is Forka-Spoonitch, if you can believe it."

"And mine is Spoonitch-Forka. We're just leaving for our honeymoon."

"This really is bad timing," Gilbert said. "It's just that our friend Manny Morgenstern found this newspaper article. Remember the medicine show that Jinny said she and Sullivan went to see? The article is about a show with the same name."

The two officers took the copy of the article and each held a corner as they read. "But this is a hundred years old," said Officer Spoonitch-Forka.

"That's the strange thing," said Gilbert. "There are people going around imitating this old medicine show."

Officer Forka-Spoonitch put her hand on Gilbert's arm. "We know how much grief you still feel. And that you'll believe anything that might mean your son is still alive. But we're police officers, not historians. We can't follow up a hundred–year-old lead."

"Which really isn't a lead at all," said Officer Spoonitch-Forka. "We're sorry. Listen, if you turn up anything else, anything at all, do call us. *After* our honeymoon, please."

Gilbert and Loretta watched as the new husband and wife got into the police car. The car drove slowly off, tin cans rattling behind. Then they closed the door.

"I'm sorry," Gilbert said to his wife.

"They don't understand. I still believe we're onto something."

Just then the doorbell rang.

"Now what?" Gilbert said, opening the door. He saw two boys standing there, both looking uncomfortable.

"Mr. and Mrs. Mintz? I'm Norval Simick."

"Of course," Loretta said. "How nice to see you."

"And I'm Samuel Patinsky. I used to bully your son."

"Really?" Gilbert said.

"But I'm sorry about it."

"Glad to hear it. Are you selling chocolate bars to raise money for the school?"

Norval shook his head. "We came to talk about Sullivan. We miss him, you see. Last year we held a celebration at school for him."

"We didn't know," Loretta said. "That's really touching."

"And this year we want to do something else," Samuel said. "We're thinking of a plaque or a statue maybe. Some kind of memorial."

Gilbert frowned. "A memorial is for dead people. Sullivan isn't dead."

"He isn't?" the two boys said at once.

"We don't think so," Loretta explained. "We believe that he was kidnapped. By a travelling medicine show."

"You aren't kidding?" Norval couldn't believe what

he was hearing. "Do you hear that, Samuel? Sullivan is alive!"

"Unbelievable!"

The two boys began to jump crazily around, shouting, "He's alive, he's alive!"

Loretta and Gilbert looked at each other. "I think we'd better ask them in," Loretta said.

❋

Jinny and Manny sat on a concrete bench outside a stone building that had the words *Tuliana Town Hall* chiselled over the door. They had come to Tuliana only because it was the next town, but they hadn't found anything.

"I'm tired all over." Jinny yawned. "My hair is tired. My ears are tired. My big toes are tired."

"That makes two of us," Manny said, his eyes closed. "It's hard being on the road day after day. Sleeping in a different bed, or on a different piece of ground. Not seeing your mom and dad."

"I miss them." Yawn again.

"I bet you do. Very few kids could have lasted even this long. Sullivan would be proud of you."

"*Will* be proud of me. Because I'm going to find him and you're going to tell him that I'm the greatest sister anyone ever had."

"Yes, I am."

Manny leaned his chin in his hand. Even before Jinny spoke, he'd been trying to decide what to do. At the very least, Manny thought, they needed a break from this life of sleeping bags. He leaned over to open a pocket on his backpack and drew out a notebook with pink flowers on the cover (it had been a present from Jinny).

"Let me see. Yes, I was right. Do you remember the parents of the boy with the dogs? The Samartinos?"

"Uh-huh."

"They gave us the address of some cousins, also called Samartino. It turns out they live in the next town over. They said we could stay any time. It might be a good idea to rest up in a real house and have some people to talk to."

Jinny pushed herself closer to Manny. "What if they're not nice people?"

"Then we can just say we're passing by. We don't have to stay. Okay?"

"Okay."

"It'll take us almost an hour to walk there, I'm afraid. We'd better get started."

Jinny groaned. But she got up and hefted her pack onto her back. Manny helped her to adjust the straps and then put on his own. They picked up their canes and the old man and the young girl began to walk down the road.

By the time they approached the address, night was coming on. The old brick house stood a little crookedly, with later additions built onto it in a haphazard fashion so that it sprawled out to the sides and back. Scattered about the front yard were scooters, bikes, pails, an old birdcage, a rubber boot, and a scarecrow made from a plastic pumpkin head and a body of straw-stuffed clothing.

"I don't like the scarecrow," Jinny said, clinging to Manny. "I once saw a scary movie on TV. These teen-agers had to go up to a house just like this one. There was a man in the house wearing a mask."

"What happened?" asked Manny.

"I don't know. Sullivan came in and made me turn it off. It gave me nightscares."

"You mean nightmares."

"No, I mean night*scares*."

"You stay beside me."

"Okay. But be prepared to *run*."

They came up to the door. A scrap of paper was taped to the frosted glass. *Bell broken. Knock LOUD.* Manny knocked.

The door opened. Sure enough, just as in Jinny's movie, a person in a mask appeared. Only the person was a child smaller than Jinny and the mask was of a pussycat. In the child's hand was a half-eaten banana.

"Hi!" chirped the small, masked person. "You want to come in and play with us?"

"I . . . I think so," Jinny said.

Behind the pussycat another person appeared, a couple of inches taller and wearing a pirate's hat and an eye patch. "Who are you?" asked the pirate.

"I'm Jinny. This is my friend Manny."

A third and a fourth and a fifth child appeared behind the first two. One had her face painted with stars, one wore round black glasses and had a pretend scar on his forehead, and one had an arm in a sling and red paint on his cheek meant to look like blood.

"We're having chicken pot pie for dinner," said the girl with painted stars.

"I love chicken pot pie," Jinny replied.

"That's good," said the smallest child in the pussycat mask. She pulled down the mask and smiled, showing two missing teeth. "Come on!" She pulled a giggling Jinny into the house and a moment later all the children were pounding up the stairs.

Manny stood in the doorway, not sure what to do. The kids had asked Jinny in but they hadn't asked *him* in. He called into the house. "Hello? *Hello?*"

A woman was just passing with a basket of laundry.

"Oh," she said, pushing the hair back over her ear. "Can I help you?"

"I hope so. We're looking for a boy named Sullivan Mintz. He disappeared several months ago. And some other children as well, including your nephew, Matthew."

"Of course you are!" cried the woman, and she put down the basket and surprised Manny by giving him a hug. "It's wonderful, what you're doing. Our family has just been devastated by Matthew going missing. Come in, come in. We're about to sit down for dinner. Eddy!" she shouted behind her. "Set two more plates!"

What happened after that seemed so wonderful to both Manny and Jinny that for a long time afterward, they would talk about it to renew their spirits. They were swept up into the life of the Samartinos, into the warm, disorderly house with its overloaded bookshelves and wooden tubs brimming with well-used toys, and old musical instruments hanging on the walls.

In the dining room a long table was crowded with plates and glasses, pitchers of milk and juice, bowls of pickles and celery sticks, and three big, steaming chicken pot pies that smelled delicious. For a long time now, Jinny and Manny had eaten their meals together, talking in low voices or not speaking at all. But here was a dinner so noisy people had to shout to be heard.

The kids ate and drank and laughed and told jokes and broke into silly songs and poked one another and complained and asked for seconds. Meanwhile, Mr. and Mrs. Samartino treated Manny and Jinny like visiting royalty. They insisted Manny put on a pair of warm slippers. They poured him a glass of beer. They heaped Jinny's plate with food.

When dinner was over, the kids cleared the table in record time. The girl with the pussycat mask, which was now pushed on top of her head, announced a game of Boinga. "Jinny can play Boinga with us!" she declared.

"Sure," Jinny said, jumping alongside them. "What's Boinga?"

"We made it up," said the boy pirate. "It's a combination of hide-and-seek, tennis, and relay-racing."

"With squirt guns," added the girl with stars on her face.

While they played, the Samartinos insisted on giving Manny the "royal treatment." Mr. Samartino was a licensed massage therapist and took Manny into the back room where his table was set up. He worked out all the aches and pains in the old man's tired body. Then Mrs. Samartino drew him a hot bath with soothing lavender salts and Manny soaked for a long time with his eyes closed.

He wrapped himself in a soft robe and came out of the bathroom. Smelling cinnamon, he saw Mrs. Samartino approach with a piece of freshly baked apple cake.

Jinny ran up. "You know what the kids are going to do next?" she said breathlessly. "They're going to crawl out of a window and onto the roof and then jump onto the trampoline in the backyard!"

Mrs. Samartino handed the apple cake to Manny. "No, Jinny," she said, hurrying down the hall, "they're not."

After Mrs. Samartino put a stop to that, she and her husband got the kids to take their own baths and get into pyjamas and brush their teeth and settle into bed. Jinny was happy to share a bed with the pussycat girl.

Manny went in to say good night. The Samartino girls had already fallen asleep but Jinny's eyes were open and shining.

Manny kneeled down to whisper, "I'm glad you had such a good time. So did I."

"I love them all," she whispered back. "I love this girl the best but I can't remember her name."

"It won't be easy going back on the road."

Jinny's face turned serious. Manny was her most favourite old person in the world, but it wasn't the same as having kids to play with. But she said, "We have to find Sullivan. And the other kids, too. That's the most important thing."

"Yes, but I don't think it would hurt if we stayed for another day. The Samartinos think we need it and I'm inclined to agree. Would that be all right with you?"

"All right?" Jinny yelped and then covered her mouth, not wanting to wake the other girl up. "That would be fantastic times five!"

"All right, then." Manny leaned over and kissed her on the forehead. He stood up and breathed deeply. He hadn't felt this good in weeks. He was going to say good night to Jinny, but when he looked down, he saw that she was already asleep.

❉ 9 ❉

THE WIGGLING SACK

 HE swamp was choked with weird, curling plants the likes of which Sullivan had never seen before. Giant lily pads lay like green plates on the surface while clouds of algae floated just below.

Sullivan squinched up his nose in disgust at another wave of swamp smell. Once again, it was hard to understand why Master Melville had chosen this place to perform the show. With breakfast over, the other performers were feeling the spongy ground under their feet or touching the layer of moss that grew on the trees. Sullivan felt as if they were sailors on the old ships that went exploring for months and years—to the South Sea Islands, South America, China. The tropical landscapes felt weird and foreign; the only things familiar to them were the bunks they slept on, the pots they cooked in, and each other.

"Dexter! Come over here."

Esmeralda was calling him. He walked over to where she stood at the edge of the swamp with a stick in her hand. The smell there was even worse.

"Ach! How can you stand right here? It's revolting."

"Dex, do you see that burlap sack in the water?" She kept her eyes on whatever she was looking at.

"Where?" Sullivan shaded his brow. Floating against some lily pads he saw a sack with the words *Happy Bake Flour* on it. "Yup, I see it. It's definitely a sack."

"I know it's a sack. Look closer. Do you see it *moving*?"

Sullivan kept watching. Sure enough, the sack twitched. "There might be a frog under it," he said. The sack fluttered a couple of times and grew still. He kept watching but it didn't move again.

"Something's weird. I think you should check it out."

"Me?"

"I'd do it but it might be a snake. Or a giant water spider. I have a thing about both."

Did she think Sullivan *liked* sneaking up on snakes and spiders? Still, he recognized an opportunity to show how brave he was, even if, in fact, he wasn't. So Sullivan took Esmeralda's stick and began to edge closer to the water, trying not to get his running shoes wet. He stepped from a stone to a log and hovered there.

"The stink is unbearable. I might keel over."

"That sack has completely stopped moving. We have to open it."

He wanted to ask why they had to open it but instead he took a step farther, onto another, more waterlogged branch. The branch dipped, soaking his foot in slime. But he managed to make it to the next stump and he reached out with the stick. He dragged the sack towards himself. When it got close enough, he grabbed hold of the neck of the sack and skipped back to shore.

"It's tied shut with a rope," he said. "I'm not good with knots."

"I can do it."

So Sullivan held the sack, which wasn't very heavy, while Esmeralda worked out the knot. The rope fell to the ground.

"Here goes," Sullivan said. He slowly opened the sack and the two of them peered in.

"Oh no," Esmeralda moaned.

It was a puppy. A small black puppy. And it wasn't moving.

Esmeralda reached in with both hands and pulled the puppy out. It was soaked with swamp water. "It's chilled to the bone," she said. Sullivan put his hand against its body. He could just detect a slow movement of the ribs, in and out.

"It's barely alive," he said. "Here, wrap my jacket around it."

"What was it doing in that sack?"

"I think somebody was trying to get rid of it. By drowning."

"That's just sick. The poor thing, I can feel it trembling. What should we do?" asked Esmeralda.

"I don't know, but Clarence will."

They began to walk quickly towards the caravan, all the while calling for Clarence to hurry over. And Clarence, who had been sitting with Snoot, heard the panic in their voices and came on the run.

"What is it? What have you got?"

Esmeralda held out the bundle. "It might die. We don't know what to do."

Frederick, too, came up to see what the shouting was about. Esmeralda pulled away the jacket to reveal the puppy's tiny head. Its eyes were closed and the tip of its tongue stuck out.

"Give it here," Clarence said and carefully took the bundle into his arms. "I'm going to get it properly dry. Start a fire and warm up some milk. I hope it's not too late."

"Looks like a goner to me," Frederick said. But Sullivan hurried to start the fire and Esmeralda went to get the milk. Master and Mistress Melville didn't approach, but watched from the side of the caravan. Clarence came over to the fire, the dry puppy now wrapped in his own towel, and sat on a chair. The animal, a male, shuddered, as if having a bad dream.

The milk was ready but Clarence said the puppy was too weak to drink. He held him on his lap for half an hour and then asked them to heat the milk up again. He touched his finger to the milk and put it to the puppy's mouth. After a moment the tip of the pink tongue touched it. He got another drop. For a long while Clarence fed the puppy this way, a drop or two at a time, its eyes always closed.

"That's good, isn't it?" asked Esmeralda.

"Yes, but I still don't know. He won't take any more, he's too exhausted. He needs to sleep."

Clarence did not move from his spot near the fire. Snoot stood by him and looked up at the puppy, which was still wrapped in the towel, making the occasional quiet whimper. Finally she lay down at Clarence's feet.

In the early afternoon, Master Melville made a cup of tea and gave it to Sullivan to take to Clarence. Clarence kept one hand around the bundle while he held the cup with the other and drank.

"That's good."

They looked down at the puppy. He opened his eyes. And closed them again.

"Did you see that?" Sullivan asked.

"Let's keep our voices down."

The puppy opened his eyes again. Without moving, he looked up at Clarence.

"Hello, little thing," Clarence cooed. He stroked the puppy's head with a finger. "I think he wagged his tail, or tried to, anyway. Maybe he's going to be all right after all."

Sullivan hurried to tell the others. Clarence couldn't sit any longer so Esmeralda took his place and, after her, Sullivan. It became time to make dinner, which Clarence ate with the puppy in his lap. Then the others cleaned up and prepared the stage for the evening show. Master Melville came by Clarence in his chair to tell him that he could miss the performance that night.

"So it looks like the little scamp will survive,"

Master Melville said to Sullivan as the two of them walked towards the stage.

"Clarence thinks so. It's a good thing that Esmeralda spotted that sack. I guess we really did save that puppy."

"More to the point," Master Melville said, "you may have saved Clarence."

Within two days, the puppy was running about and tripping over his own paws. He learned to drink from a bowl and eat dog food softened with milk. When Clarence scratched him behind the ears, saying, "Good little dog," he wagged his tail so hard that his whole backside moved.

At first, Clarence kept Snoot at a distance, afraid that she might become jealous. But as the puppy gained strength, he introduced them by holding the squirming creature in his arms while bending down to the older dog. Snoot came up, whimpering a little, sniffed the puppy, and then licked his nose. After that, Snoot wanted to be near him every moment. As the puppy grew bolder and began exploring more, she stayed with him to make sure he didn't get lost. When the puppy grew tired, she curled around him and the two slept together.

The puppy needed a name. They all discussed the

question at dinner, the two dogs resting by Clarence's feet.

"How about Blackie?" Frederick suggested.

"That's not exactly imaginative," Clarence responded.

"You could name him after my favourite singer," Esmeralda said, "Elvis."

"He's a dog, not the king of rock and roll."

"I kind of like Bandit," Sullivan offered.

"Too corny."

Master Melville cleared his throat. "If I might venture an opinion, why not give the creature a name that speaks of a great destiny? I propose Caesar. Don't you agree, dearest?"

Until now, Mistress had been silent. She had always been quiet at dinner, but since the death of Snit, she had not spoken once while they were at the table. Now she said, "Let the boy decide for himself."

"Actually, I like Caesar," Clarence said. "That's a good boy, Caesar." The puppy's wagging tail smacked Snoot in the face, but Snoot didn't seem to mind.

Of course, Caesar was too young to train, but Clarence began talking about how he might soon become part of the act. Maybe he could get Snoot to coax the puppy across the stage or up a little ramp or into a box. He began making sketches on paper, stick-figure dogs with arrows going in different directions. In the meantime, his good spirits returned and he became the easygoing Clarence that Sullivan had always depended on for cheering up. Snoot, too, was clearly happier. She was vigilant in watching over the young dog but she played, too, as if learning to be a puppy again.

☀ 10 ☀

SMALL ENOUGH

THE wagon rolled through the night, Soggy Biscuit's hooves making dull thuds on the earthen path. High overhead, the tiny lights of an airplane blinked in the night sky. Master Melville looked up as if he were seeing some visitor from a future world.

"Are you sure this is the right way?" Mistress Melville sniffed.

"Absolutely, my radish. This is a road—or at least it was a hundred years ago." He gave the reins a shake. "I must say, that was very clever of you. I never would have thought of it. I'm simply not devious enough."

Mistress Melville sniffed again. "I could hardly count on you to improve the situation."

"But to buy that puppy and then put it in the sack and throw it into the swamp! Just where it might be seen. If the girl had noticed it a moment later, the poor thing would have perished."

"So? I would simply have bought another."

"Yes, but I would never have thought to let *them* find it."

"Do you think they would have accepted it directly from me?" Mistress said. "The boy—Clarence—hates me. They all do."

"Hate is a very strong word, my dear."

"It is the appropriate word."

"Certainly Frederick doesn't hate you. He rather worships you. Perhaps if you showed him the occasional kindness . . ."

"For what purpose? Don't ask me to do what I can't."

"Of course, my buttercup."

They travelled on. Dense trees on either side of the path hemmed in the caravan.

"We do still have the small problem of being short an act," Master Melville mused. "Five just seems to work as the perfect number. We sell the most bottles with five. Not using Napoleon is a real shame. And of course it was in the original."

"Then we must find someone who can operate it."

"That's going to be exceedingly difficult. The person must be small enough and also clever at chess. Remember how long it took us to find Clarence? The dogs were a bonus. Such children don't grow on trees."

"Wait," Mistress said suddenly.

"Wait for what, my zucchini flower?"

"Do try not to speak for a moment, if that's possible. I'm thinking."

"Absolutely, dearest, I won't say a word. But what are you thinking?"

She shook her head impatiently. "A memory. A memory is stirring in my mind. Be silent while I try to retrieve it."

On they rode. Master Melville, who found silence difficult, began to hum but stopped himself. Instead, he began to bite a nail.

"That girl," Mistress said. "That annoying girl."

"What girl?"

"It happened not long after we acquired the juggling boy. At a performance there was a small girl. She approached Clarence and the other one—Dexter. She told them that she was the chess champion of her school. She was a minuscule thing, an easy fit into the contraption. Clarence tried to give her a letter. That's why I chained him in that cemetery."

"That *was* rather harsh. But I don't understand what you are proposing."

"You can be so dense. We shall kidnap her."

"Kidnap her? We'd have to go back hundreds of miles. You don't even know her name."

"We need that girl."

"Yes, yes, but should we not keep our eye on the prize? The reason we're doing this at all? We must move forward—"

"She said her name to the boys but I didn't catch it. I do remember, though, what town we were just outside. If we can find out her name, then we can lure her to the show. We need to squeeze it out of one of them."

Master Melville sighed. "So it's decided, is it? I must try and find out her name."

"Not you. You'll just botch it. I will find out. Clarence won't give anything away, he's too wary. But the other one—Dexter—he's another matter. Now hurry us up. Whip that horse, I'm tired of this endless ride."

"Tallyho, my dear." Master Melville brandished the whip, cracking it on the horse's flank. The animal whinnied and began to trot. Overhead, the blinking lights were gone. There was only darkness.

11

A PRIVATE AUDIENCE

$\mathcal{S}$ALERNO. Rastelli. Brunn. These were the great jugglers of the past. But how long had it been since Sullivan had lain on his own bed, dreaming of one day having the nerve to perform in front of the old people of the Stardust Home? Now he went on stage every night. He had, in his small way, joined the fraternity of professional jugglers. And yet it was a long time since their greatness had inspired him. Frederick was right, being an artist meant more than just throwing stuff into the air. Salerno, Rastelli, and Brunn all had a mesmerizing presence on the stage, and an act that didn't merely entertain but excited, thrilled, and moved audiences.

From the prop trunk, Sullivan managed to scrounge up a black bowler hat. It took him a few days to learn how to roll the hat on its brim, down his arm to his fingers, and then back again. Or catch it on the toe of his shoe and kick it up in the air, catching it on his head. Not to mention balancing it on his nose.

Juggling a hat wasn't going to make him an artist. But it would help to freshen up his act. And Frederick had sparked an idea in him when he had mentioned Charlie Chaplin. Sure, Sullivan already had a character of sorts: the accidental juggler. But what if, in keeping with the old-fashioned quality of the medicine show, he set his act in the past? For some time now he'd been brooding on the idea of a real character, sort of a cross between Charlie Chaplin's Little Tramp (he had watched the old silent movies with his father) and the Artful Dodger from *Oliver Twist* (his mother had read him the book). A street kid trying to survive. A boy who begged for a crust of bread, who maybe even had to steal to keep from starving. A boy who might learn to juggle in order to earn money and survive. The idea wasn't clear, nothing was worked out, but he felt excited by the possibilities.

Sullivan was attempting to catch the hat behind his back when he noticed Mistress watching him as she ate a peach. She was dressed in one of her daytime outfits—a black silk blouse and tight black slacks and black boots. The sight of her watching him unnerved Sullivan so much that he missed catching the bowler.

Mistress wiped her lips with a finger. Then she threw the peach away and approached him.

"You are becoming ambitious," she said. "Wanting to improve."

"I guess we all are."

"But you have something special. A gift."

"Oh, I don't know." Sullivan looked down at his own shoes.

"We've never had a proper chat, just you and I. Why don't you come into the caravan with me? We can get to know one another."

"You mean, *your* side of the caravan?"

"Unless you've got something better to do."

"No, nothing at all."

"Come along, then."

Sullivan looked around to see if any of the other kids had noticed, but they were all busy doing something else. He followed her to the caravan, where she stepped up to the seat. Behind it was the small door leading to the Melvilles' side of the interior. None of them had ever gone through that door and they had often speculated about what it was like. A cross between a royal bedroom and a luxury hotel was how they had imagined it.

"After you," Mistress said, opening the door.

Sullivan climbed up quickly and ducked his head as he went in. Mistress followed, closing the door after her. She turned up an oil lamp.

Whatever Sullivan was expecting, this was definitely not it. For one thing, the space was small, less than half that of their own side. There were small leather sofas facing each other that looked as if they folded out to become a bed. The leather was worn and several tears had been sewn up with heavy thread. An end table had been made from an old wooden box. On it sat a ceramic jug and a couple of chipped mugs. A small shelf held some musty books and an old album or scrapbook. There was a rag rug on the floor. And that was it. The Melvilles' quarters weren't luxurious at all. They were cramped and dreary. Why would anyone choose to live this way?

"Sit down," Mistress said in an almost kindly voice. He perched on a sofa, feeling the springs sigh beneath him, while she sat opposite. "Yes, this is our little home. I can see by the look on your face that you were expecting more."

"No, not at all."

"We, too, make sacrifices for our art. Of course, we do like to have what little comforts we can." She picked up the jug, pulled the cork, and poured a golden liquid into one of the mugs. "Have a taste," she said, handing it to him.

"I'm not very thirsty."

"Oh, it won't hurt. Drink up."

Sullivan put the mug to his lips. The liquid had a lovely, honey sort of smell. He took a sip and felt a sweet warmth move down his throat.

"It's delicious." He emptied his mug.

"I'm so glad you like it. Have a sip more." She leaned over and poured again. "I think it's good to have a little time together on our own, don't you? I'd like to know you better."

"You would?"

"Why not? A talented and handsome boy like you."

Sullivan leaned back on the sofa. Somehow his mug was empty again. His insides felt all warm and he could barely keep from closing his eyes. He hadn't felt this peaceful in a long time.

"So many good times we've had," Mistress went on. "Like that time the magician, Frederick, spilled an entire pot of soup before dinner."

"You called him a clumsy ape," Sullivan murmured.

"Did I? Yes, we've had a lot of fun. Do you remember the time a small girl came up to you and Clarence? He wanted to give her a letter to mail. She told you she was her school chess champion."

"You left Clarence in a cemetery for it."

"Do we always have to remember the bad? She was such a smart girl. Now, what was her name again. Topsy? Georgina?"

Sullivan's eyelids fluttered. He felt the sofa sway gently beneath him, like a canoe rocking in the waves. "Not Topsy or Georgina," he yawned. "Lilly. Lilly Reilly."

No sooner had he spoken than Sullivan felt himself being yanked by his shirt collar. He saw the little door open, heard Mistress say, "The party's over," and felt a boot shove him from behind. Suddenly he was down on all fours in the dust.

Sullivan dusted himself off. What a weirdo that Mistress was, he thought. Asking him in one moment and throwing him out the next. His head felt so foggy. What did she ask him? Oh yes, something about that girl.

And then his head cleared and he understood. *"Oh no,"* he said aloud. What had he done?

❈

Sullivan hardly said a word at dinner, and his performance that night was competent at best. The last bottle
of Hop-Hop Drops was sold and Master Melville
urged the performers to pack up the caravan as quickly
as possible.

"Hurry up!" He clapped his hands. "We've got no
time to lose." Before long they were in their pyjamas
listening to the lock click shut from inside their
beds. Soggy Biscuit snorted and the caravan began to
move.

"Come on, Dex," Clarence said in the dark. "You've
been quiet all day. You've got to tell us what was up
with you and the Black Death. I thought I was hallu-
cinating when I saw you coming out of the Melvilles'
quarters."

"What's it really like in there?" Esmeralda
wondered. "Is it all gold brocade and velvet upholstery
and glittering mirrors?"

"It doesn't make sense," Frederick complained. "If
she was going to take in anyone, then it should have
been me. As usual I get treated like dirt."

"Don't pick on Dexter," Clarence said. "It's not
his fault if the Black Death decided to be nice for a
change. But tell us, Dex, what's going on?"

Sullivan lay on his bunk, his blanket pulled up to
his chin. It was too dark to see but he stared up towards

the invisible ceiling. "I think maybe something *is* my fault," he said at last. "Mistress tricked me."

"She's good at that," Esmeralda said. "What did she do?"

"She got me inside and treated me all nice. She gave me something to drink. I don't know what it was, but it made me feel funny. And then she started asking me about that time a girl came up to me and Clarence. Do you remember her, Clarence?"

"How could I forget after what the Black Death did to me? Her name was Lilly."

"Lilly Reilly," Sullivan said miserably. "The whole thing was a trap. She wanted me to tell her Lilly's name."

"But you didn't tell her, right?"

Sullivan didn't answer.

"Oh, Dexter," Esmeralda said.

"She was really devious and clever about it. I hardly even knew what happened."

"Don't feel so bad," Clarence said quickly. "That woman could trick a tiger out of its stripes."

"Anyway," Frederick said, "I don't see what she wants the name for."

"I figured it out after. Lilly would be perfect to operate Napoleon. She's even smaller than Clarence used to be. And she's good at chess."

"Okay," Clarence said. "I admit that makes sense. But it's not as if they can just call her up on the phone. *Hello? Lilly Reilly? Would you like to leave your family forever and join our insane medicine show?* She's far behind us. We're going in the other direction."

"That's right," Esmeralda agreed. "We're heading south. And this caravan doesn't exactly go fast. It operates on Soggy power. You know what I think? I think the Black Death was trying to mess with your head. She can spot our weaknesses the way a hawk spots a mouse."

"I wish you'd all shut up," Frederick growled. "I want to go to sleep."

"Maybe nothing will happen," Sullivan said. "I'll try not to let it get to me."

"Good," Esmeralda said.

They stopped talking. The only sounds were the creaking boards of the caravan and the jingling of Soggy's harness. Sullivan closed his eyes and tried to sleep, but his thoughts were too anxious and it was almost an hour before he finally drifted off.

Almost immediately—or so it felt—something jarred him awake. The caravan had come to a halt.

"Why have we stopped?" came Clarence's drowsy voice.

Lying on the floor next to Snoot, Caesar began to

whimper. Clarence let his arm drop over the side of the bunk to pet him. "That's okay, Caesar, nothing to worry about."

"This doesn't feel right," Frederick said in a low voice. "They're up to something."

Sullivan heard the key jiggling in the lock. The door of the caravan swung open.

"Everyone up," Melville said. "File out, quick as bunnies. There isn't a moment to lose. Leave the dogs inside."

Sullivan pulled off his blanket and got up. He put on his running shoes and followed Frederick out the door. In the dark he could just make out a small wooden building beside them.

"It looks like an old railway station," Clarence said.

"An abandoned one," Frederick added. "See how the windows are broken and the door is missing? Looks like it hasn't been used in decades."

"Quiet, all of you," Mistress barked. "Stay where you are and don't move until told otherwise."

They stood there in their pyjamas. Five minutes, ten. Sullivan looked more closely at the small station, many of its roof shingles blown off. A rat scurried out through the open doorway. Fifteen minutes, twenty. Soggy Biscuit stamped a hoof. The wind picked up.

"You said it was all arranged," Mistress hissed.

"It is, my fruitcake. Should be just another minute or two."

"It better be."

"Listen! I hear it now."

Sullivan strained to hear. He could just make out a low rumble.

"It's a train," Esmeralda whispered. "But why are we waiting for a train?"

"They must be taking us back—" Clarence began, until he was silenced by a cuff on the back of his head from Mistress.

"I said be quiet!"

The rumble grew louder until it became the unmistakable sound of iron wheels on rails. A long and plaintive whistle blew. Another long moment of waiting and then the enormous engine appeared slowly past the last trees. The train rolled along the tracks, brakes screeching as car after car passed them. It slowed to a crawl until the train finally stopped.

"Sullivan, Frederick, come and help me," demanded Master Melville.

The two boys followed as he ran along the train to a particular freight car. A large *X* had been chalked on the metal door. "Grab hold and pull," Master Melville said, and they all grabbed the door. Grunting with the effort, they slid it open.

Master Melville climbed into the car and then slid out a wide ramp until the end rested on the ground. He walked back down.

"My dearest, if you would lead the horse up the ramp. The rest of us will push the caravan from behind."

"I won't do it," Sullivan said. "I won't help."

"You'll help, all right," Mistress said. "Or I'll beat this horse. I'll beat it to death if I have to."

"You wouldn't!" Esmeralda cried. But Mistress held up the whip as if to deliver a blow. So the four of them got behind the caravan, where Master Melville was already waiting. He called out, "Push!" and they leaned their shoulders against the back while Mistress urged on the horse. The caravan moved slowly up the ramp, Soggy's hooves clanging on the metal.

"Lazy good-for-nothings!" Mistress cried. "Push harder!"

Sullivan leaned into the caravan, his muscles burning with the effort. One more big push and it was in.

"Now everyone get inside," Master Melville said.

They climbed the ramp into the dark freight car. It smelled of dry cow manure. Master Melville had Frederick help him pull up the ramp and then they slid the door closed.

The train whistle blew. The car shuddered and began to move.

"I'm not going to let you," Sullivan said. "I'm not going to let you kidnap Lilly Reilly."

"Lock them back inside the caravan," Mistress said dismissively. "I've had enough of them for a while."

* 12 *

TRAP

◯HE train sped through the countryside. That's how it felt to Sullivan, who had known only the steady gait of Soggy Biscuit for so long. Every few hours the caravan's back door would open and Master Melville would pass in some hunks of bread and cheese, a bag of apples, a jar of water. They would share their food with the dogs. They had only Clarence's stub of a candle for light, and when it burned out, they could only doze on their bunks, losing track of time, until they didn't know if it was day or night.

Twice the train stopped. One by one the performers

were allowed to go into the bushes. Sullivan thought about making a run for it then. But even if he managed to reach the police, he couldn't have told them where the kidnapping was going to take place. The only way he could be sure of thwarting the Melvilles was to be there when it happened.

"This is all my fault," Sullivan said back inside the caravan. "If only I hadn't given up Lilly Reilly's name."

"Yeah," Clarence said. "And if only you hadn't taken up juggling. Or gone to see the medicine show. If only the Black Death didn't have a heart made of coal. If only Master Melville didn't have delusions of grandeur."

"Clarence is totally right," Esmeralda said. "It isn't your fault."

"Even I have to admit that's true," Frederick agreed.

"All I know is that I'm going to make sure it doesn't happen. I'm not going to let them get her."

"I've been thinking the same thing," Clarence said.

"Make that three of us," Esmeralda put in.

"There's going to be some ugly consequences if you mess up their plans," Frederick said.

Sullivan lay down, pulling up his blanket even though he was now dressed. They all were—they had decided they'd better be ready for anything, and clothes were better than pyjamas. It was definitely getting colder. He fell asleep, woke up, needed to pee, made himself sleep again. The screeching of the train wheels woke him. He and the others felt about for their shoes and jackets and sat waiting.

The caravan door opened. "Come on, hurry up now. We've got to get the caravan down the ramp. Quick, before the train starts moving!"

They slid open the freight car door and let in the blinding sun. Sullivan guarded his eyes until they adjusted enough that he could look out. A thin layer of snow covered the fields.

"No wonder I'm so cold," Esmeralda said.

They put down the ramp and then Mistress led Soggy Biscuit down. This time the performers had to make sure that the caravan didn't roll down so quickly that it smashed at the bottom. The ramp went up again, and even as they were sliding the car door shut, the train started to move. They watched as it picked up steam, the whistle piercing the cold air.

"Back in the caravan," Master Melville instructed. "We've only got a few miles to go, and then we'll cook ourselves a nice hot meal."

It was less than half an hour before they were let out again. The caravan had come to rest in a field, autumn's cornstalks sticking up out of the snow. Behind them some woods began.

They put on all the layers of clothing they had and got a fire going. Master Melville rode off on Soggy Biscuit and came back with eggs, sausages, bread and jam, coffee and milk. They each got a big plate and ate hungrily, warming their insides.

Sullivan whispered to Clarence next to him, "Do you recognize this place?"

"We've been to so many, most of them have blended together. And the snow changes things too."

"Maybe Lilly Reilly has moved away. Maybe she's in bed with the flu or on a school trip."

"Anything's possible. When you get right down to it, the chances of her coming are pretty slim."

Master Melville let them gather branches to keep the fire going. He went into the caravan and came out again in his overalls and straw hat, a bunch of handbills in a bag on his shoulder. Once more he mounted Soggy Biscuit and trotted off. Mistress sat on a stool by the caravan, keeping her eye on them.

"Why are you lazing about?" she said at last. "People need somewhere to sit. You've got to clear the snow away from the front of the stage. Go on, now."

Esmeralda looked at Sullivan and shrugged as she got up.

"It's too cold out," he said. "Nobody's going to want

to stand around and watch a show." But they began clearing the ground.

Master Melville returned. The stage was set, the props were in place, and with the sun quickly going down, the performers waited in the wings. Sullivan kept his hands in his pockets. He was worried that his fingers would be too stiff to juggle—if anyone actually showed up. Which, at the moment, looked extremely doubtful.

Master Melville stepped onto the stage so he could see the performers in the wings on either side. "I have something to say before tonight's performance," he began. "I know these last days have been stressful. And I know that the four of you have some concerns about what we're doing. But I want to assure you that this is all for the best. The show must go on, you see. And for it to go on, we need—well, trust Mistress and myself to know what we need. The best, the *only* thing for you to do is perform tonight to the best of your ability."

"Oh, what rot," Mistress said. Musical instruments strapped to her like armour, she pushed her way onto the stage. "Let's be crystal clear. If any of you try to mess with our plan, you will live to regret it. Not just for yourself but for all the others as well. And for what? To save some girl you don't even know? Do not get above your station. Do not think that you understand how the events of this world are supposed to unfold." She pushed aside one curtain. "Now, to your places. I see the first mark!"

Sullivan peeked and saw a figure in hat and mitts crossing the snowy field. Behind him were three more, one with his scarf wrapped around his face. And now he could see more climbing the fence, parents holding the hands of kids in snowsuits or carrying them on their shoulders. It was unprofessional to keep looking, but he wanted to see every face that approached.

"Do you see Lilly?" Clarence asked.

"No sign of her."

Some people brought plastic sleds or squares of cardboard to sit on. Night was coming on fast and the lanterns seemed to glow brighter. Master Melville himself kept scanning the crowd, delaying the show in the hope of Lilly Reilly appearing. At last he couldn't wait any longer and signalled to Mistress, who began to play "Ukulele Lady." He strode onto the stage, did a little soft-shoe dance, doffed his hat, and began to speak.

"Welcome, ladies and gentlemen, children of all ages. It is an honour to present to you our humble entertainment."

His eyes narrowed and a little smile crossed his face.

Sullivan looked out. A latecomer was sitting down at the side of the front row. From this angle he couldn't see her face behind the hood of her parka. *Please,* he prayed silently, *don't let it be Lilly Reilly. Let it be anyone but her.* Then the girl turned her head.

The same bangs, the same big eyes shining brightly with excitement. It *was* Lilly Reilly.

Master Melville announced, "I give you . . . Frederick!"

The curtain opened and Frederick began his act. As Master Melville passed Sullivan in the wings, he spoke under his breath. "Be smart, Dexter, and everything will be fine."

Sullivan watched Frederick grab an umbrella from the air. "I was hoping for some flowers," he said. "I wonder which are the most beautiful? Roses? Orchids?" This wasn't Frederick's usual patter, so Sullivan paid more attention. The magician held up the umbrella and tossed it into the air, but now it became a handful of flowers that scattered to the stage. "Ah, lilies," he sighed, stooping to pick them up. "But it is much more difficult to bring one back after it has disappeared." He held the flowers in one hand, pulled out one bloom, and tossed it right at Lilly Reilly. But before it reached her, the flower turned into confetti.

The audience clapped, Lilly loudest of all. It was

a pretty trick, but Sullivan could see by her big smile that she hadn't got the hint. Frederick had been too subtle.

Next came Esmeralda. While balanced on the tightrope, a glass of water on her head, she looked straight at Lilly and recited a poem.

> *Looks can be deceiving, as everyone knows.*
> *And not everything that goes in, also out goes.*
> *If you look for deeper meaning in my little poem*
> *You'll find that what it says is*
> *"There's no place like home."*

Sullivan moaned inwardly. Essy's message was even more obscure! Lilly shouted "Bravo!" when Esmeralda drank the glass of water and somersaulted off the rope.

The one who *did* understand was Mistress Melville. She blew furiously on her kazoo so that Master Melville looked at her and then she nodded. He bounded up onto the stage, bowing deeply from the waist.

"Ladies and gentlemen, boys and girls. We do love to perform in nature's own theatre—the great outdoors, in other words. But tonight *is* rather frigid. I'm afraid we're going to have to shorten our show. But in order to make it up to you, I myself will perform a very special illusion. I will need a volunteer, someone who doesn't mind having her molecules dissolved so that she might travel through space."

As he spoke, Master Melville himself wheeled out a black wooden box about the size of a small coffin. The Vanishing Box! Master Melville opened the lid and knocked on all the sides to show that it was real. He turned it around to show the back. Sullivan's heart seemed to drop to his knees. He had an awful memory of darkness and falling. It hadn't been used on stage since Sullivan himself had climbed inside it. He felt so ill that he had to close his eyes for a moment, and when he opened them again, Lilly Reilly was climbing onto the stage.

"Please look inside and tell the audience what you see."

Lilly Reilly looked hesitantly into the box. She smiled and then tried to put on a serious expression. Sullivan knew that she was reading words written on a piece of paper inside. She said, "I can see the moon and the stars. I can see the whole universe."

Now Master Melville asked her to step inside; now he put his hand on her head and gently but insistently pushed her down until she was lying inside it. Now he closed the lid.

"And where will the young lady appear next? London? New York? Cairo? I shall knock on the lid three times. One . . . two . . . three . . ."

And when Master Melville opened the box, it was empty. The curtain jerked closed.

Sullivan didn't consider himself a brave person, certainly not a heroic one. He knew that Lilly Reilly was trapped in the hidden compartment of the Vanishing Box. He felt the awful guilt of having given up her name. He didn't think, didn't consider his own welfare, didn't weigh the risks and the consequences. He just *moved*.

Onto the stage he ran, behind the curtain, skidding to his knees. He found the two latches for releasing the back of the hidden compartment. He reached in, felt the girl's arm, and roughly dragged her out.

"Ow, that hurts! Is the trick over?"

"Come with me! It's a trap to kidnap you! Hurry!"

He pulled her up onto her feet just as Master Melville came through the curtains. Seeing them, he reached out to grab hold of the girl. But Sullivan shoved Master Melville—shoved him with both hands, as hard as he could, so that Master Melville's feet went out from under him and he fell backward into the billowing curtain.

"You have to trust me!" Sullivan hissed.

"I do!"

He grasped Lilly's hand and started to run. Past an astonished Frederick in the wings, and behind the caravan. He headed for the woods. Lilly stumbled but recovered and kept up with him, their hands still locked.

They reached the first trees, where the snow was suddenly deeper. Here the branches were frosted with ice, like endless Christmas trees, and even in his panic Sullivan thought they looked beautiful. That was his last thought before the Black Death stepped out from behind an evergreen, swinging a cast-iron pan.

A LITTLE BOX

INSIDE the Beanfield Public Library, Loretta Mintz was hunkered down in front of the only computer, staring at the screen. She had discovered that there were hundreds of small-town newspapers now available on the Internet, but the scanned images of their faded pages were tiring on the eyes to read. So far she had found three articles about travelling shows, but none of them was about the Melvilles. Today she read the *Massawapi Messenger*. She used the mouse to move to the next page, reading more headlines.

After an hour her eyes hurt, her back ached, and

her mouth was dry. The librarian made her a cup of tea and brought her a digestive biscuit, for which Loretta was very grateful. She dipped the biscuit and drank the tea and looked out the window at the people going in and out of stores, buying bread or vegetables or earrings, living the way people were supposed to.

After two hours of fruitless searching, she looked up at the clock. "Oh, I'm late!" she said to the librarian. Packing up her things, she hurried out to the street and, making a quick turn, entered the very next door and the offices of the *Beanfield Gazette*.

When the Bard of Beanfield had begun to write again, her poems had been eagerly read once more by readers of the *Beanfield Gazette*. Aware of the tragic occurrence in the Mintz family, they no doubt read the poems with great sympathy. But that didn't stop some from writing to the editor, Maurice Broome, who had finally asked Loretta whether she might come and see him.

The newspaper wasn't big enough to have a secretary and Loretta went right into the office of the editor, who invited her to sit down. He retreated behind his own desk and was now shuffling papers about, as if looking for something. In fact—as Loretta well knew—he was trying to figure out what to say.

Maurice cleared his throat. "First of all, Mrs. Mintz,

I want to say how honoured we are to publish your poems."

"That's very kind of you. Please, call me Loretta."

"Your poems, Loretta, have always been very popular. In fact, our surveys show that they are the third most popular feature in the paper, right after the wedding announcements and the discount coupons. I want you to feel that the *Beanfield Gazette* is your home."

"Again, that's very kind."

"For example, we wouldn't want you to publish your poems in the *Greenhaven Tribune* or the *Halliwell Hound*. Because I've heard rumours. Offers of more money."

"*More* money? You don't pay me anything, Maurice. But no, I'm not planning to take my poems anywhere else."

"That's a relief, I can tell you. But let me get to the point of our meeting. We published your latest poem, Loretta. And really, even for us, it's a bit much."

"Did you get complaints?"

"Not complaints exactly. Let's call it *concern*. Our readers are worried about you. We like attention, but not of this kind. I mean, really, Loretta, take a look at your own poem." Maurice had the latest edition of the paper open on his desk. He turned it around and slid it towards her.

"All right," she said. "I'll try to read it as if somebody else wrote it." She turned the paper around and began to read to herself.

At home I have a little box
I keep beneath my bed.
Inside it's where I've put my dreams
That are broken, cracked, or dead.

Every night I close the door
And to its cold, cold lid
I place my ear and listen to
Those dreams that I have hid.

I cannot tell you what I hear,
When to that box I'm pressed.
And if you never hear their sound,
I think it's for the best.

Loretta put down the paper. "I do see what you mean," she admitted. "It's not exactly cheerful. I don't mean to upset anyone."

Maurice Broome looked relieved. "I'm sure you don't. Please don't hesitate to send us your next poem. It's just that, well, perhaps you could be funny again, at least once in a while?"

"I'll try."

"That's excellent."

"Well, I'd better get back to the Stardust Home. I'm sure Gilbert has his hands full without me."

"There's just one more thing before you go, Loretta. It's about a book."

"A book?"

"Of your poems. I think it's time to gather them up and publish them together. We can sell it through the newspaper, and in bookstores, of course. It might not sell a lot of copies but it will be good for the newspaper's reputation—to support literature, you see."

"I don't know. I've never thought about publishing a book. And right now I'm awfully occupied with trying to find my son."

"You won't have to do a thing. Just leave it to me. I'll have a contract written up—standard royalties, of course—and you can make sure it's fair and sign it. That's really all you have to do."

Loretta rose from her chair. "It might be a waste of your time and money, Maurice, but if you want to, I don't see why not."

"Thank you, Loretta. We'll put the old poems and the new ones in it. But do remember to write us something a little cheerful?"

"All right," Loretta said, heading out the door. "If I can manage to feel cheerful."

❊

At the end of lunch hour, Norval Simick and Samuel Patinsky were standing at the front door of the school with a large cardboard box at their feet. At that moment a girl came up to the door.

"Here, take a button," Norval said, pulling one from the box and handing it to her. The button was large. The girl turned it over to see a photograph of Sullivan with the words *Have You Seen Sullivan Mintz?* curving around the bottom.

"This is the kid who drowned, isn't it?" the girl said. "You held that celebration thing last year."

"Right," Samuel said. "Only he didn't drown. He's alive and out there somewhere."

"That's great," said the girl, and she pinned it to the strap of her backpack before heading into school.

"How many have we given away now?" Norval asked.

"Eighty-eight. We've only got a dozen more. I think we'd better go in before we're late for class."

"Okay," Norval agreed. "We can give out the rest after school. See you later, then."

"Sure thing."

But as soon as they stepped into school, Norval and Samuel came face to face with Principal Washburb.

"You two," the principal commanded, "into my office."

They had no choice but to follow Principal Washburb down the hall and into his office, where Mr. Luria, the gym teacher, was lounging in a chair. Immediately he jumped up.

"What are you doing here, Luria?"

"We're supposed to talk about new football uniforms."

"Not now. I've caught these two subversives at it again. They've been handing out political propaganda. It's against school board policy to display political slogans of any kind in school."

"But they're not political slogans," Samuel said. "We want people to know that Sullivan Mintz is actually alive."

"Well, if trying to make people believe that kid didn't drown isn't a political conspiracy, I don't know what is. Mr. Luria, have you seen these revolting buttons that the kids are all wearing?"

"No, I haven't. I've been looking at this catalogue of football uniforms. I really like the purple-and-white one."

"Enough with the uniforms! Just look at one of these buttons."

Principal Washburb thrust his hand into the cardboard box. "Ah!" he cried. "I got stabbed by a pin. You're also distributing dangerous goods." He carefully pulled out a button and turned it towards the gym teacher. "What do you think of this, Luria?"

"I think . . . I think . . ."

Mr. Luria's words faded away. He looked at the photograph on the button. In his mind he suddenly saw a boy getting beaned with a ball in gym class. Yes, that was Sullivan Mintz. Then he remembered that same boy juggling on stage. Where was that? Oh yes, when he went to visit his old college buddy a few weekends ago. They had watched that entertaining medicine show, and the boy had been on stage.

"What's wrong?" the principal asked. "Your face has gone white."

Mr. Luria wondered what he should do. If he admitted to seeing the boy and missing an opportunity to bring him home, he might get into trouble. Better to forget that he ever saw this Mintz.

"Yes, I agree," he said at last. "They're definitely political. Make an announcement that all teachers are to confiscate the buttons."

"Good idea, Luria. I knew you were good for something."

"But Principal Washburb!" complained Norval. "It took us three days to make them."

"Three days? Well, now you'll have a whole week of detention to think about how much time you've wasted."

Norval and Samuel looked at each other. "I guess that means we can't give the rest out," Samuel said.

✳ 14 ✳

A DIFFICULT ADJUSTMENT

LILLY Reilly kicked. Lilly Reilly screamed. During the day, she had to be watched every second. Three times in the first two days she tried to run away, but each time the Melvilles caught her and dragged her back. The third time left Master Melville with a purple eye and Mistress with a long scratch down her face.

The night of her kidnapping, they had gotten onto another train going in the opposite direction, back where they had come from, with Sullivan nursing a swollen lump where Mistress Melville had brained him with the frying pan. They'd finally hauled the caravan out of the freight car near the site of their next performance. But nothing had gone smoothly after that.

Lilly had been locked inside the caravan along with the others for the return trip. Then, during shows, Mistress had to lock Lilly in the Vanishing Box so she wouldn't escape. She had to thump and strum her instruments as loudly as possible to cover up the girl's muffled screams.

When Master Melville told Lilly that she couldn't go back to her family just yet because her father had a bad heart—just as he had once told Sullivan—she spat out her response.

"You don't know what you're talking about! My dad jogs five miles a day! He plays squash! You're a liar! And a kidnapper! And you'd better let me go!"

The only time Lilly quieted down was at dinner. For a small girl, she had a big appetite. "Keeping up my strength," she sneered.

On the fourth night, when she seemed more placid, Master Melville casually brought up the notion of her trying to operate Napoleon. She threw a bowl of chili in his face.

Master Melville built a new folding bunk for her, above Esmeralda's. Locked in the caravan, lying in their beds one night, Frederick said, "I have to admit, you really are a scrapper."

"And you're a bunch of robots. Or slaves. Or maybe just cowards."

"We're not cowards," Esmeralda said. "We've tried to escape too."

"Tried?" Lilly pretended to laugh. "You're all pathetic. I'm going to sleep now and I'd appreciate it if you lapdogs would be quiet."

"I don't blame you," Esmeralda said. "You can call us whatever you want."

"What are you, a psychiatrist? Maybe you're the ones who need a shrink. I think you like being part of this circus."

"Technically, we're not a circus," Clarence explained. "We don't use a tent or a ring. We don't have clowns . . ."

"You're *all* clowns. Now shut up or I'm coming over to smother you with my crummy excuse for a pillow."

The conversation, Sullivan thought, was like a tennis match. They lobbed easy ones over the net and Lilly smashed them back at their heads. He admired her resistance even as he felt the sting of guilt. Why had Sullivan believed all the same lies when he'd first arrived? Why had he been so easy to manipulate, so eager to belong? Lilly was a whole other story. She even refused to answer to any new name that Master Melville came up with for her. Her strength made Sullivan burn with shame.

Dinner the next night was spaghetti, since Master Melville could hardly spare the time to shop for fear that Lilly would make another run for it. They sat around the table, eating and not talking, until Master Melville began to speak.

"Our new friend, Lilly, has certainly caused a lot of commotion. Nothing like shaking up complacency and routine, I say. We have to thank Lilly's arrival for that."

"I didn't *arrive*," Lilly said. "I was locked in a box and taken against my will."

"In any case, we are delighted to have you to complete our pentagon of young talents. But it is time for all of us to direct this energy, rather than allowing it to fly off in all directions. To direct it into our performances. Isn't that right, Eudora?"

"Just get on with it," Mistress said.

"We have decided on something that we believe will make life easier for us all, something that will help the five of you to focus your attention."

"You're letting us go?" Lilly asked. "I hope you let that horse go, too. I don't think he likes either of you any more than I do."

"Always the joker. No, we've thought of something better. If any one of you escapes, we will simply replace you. With one of your brothers or sisters."

"What?" Sullivan gasped.

Master Melville continued. "You have a little sister, don't you, Dexter? I'm sure she has some natural talent of her own. You've seen how we went back to get Lilly. We can do it for your sister, too. Or for one of yours, Clarence. Or for yours, Esmeralda and Lilly. You see, we know where your families live and much more. It's true that Frederick has no brothers and sisters, so if he goes, we'll have to take one from the others. I don't think you'd wish to do that to your friends, would you, Freddy? Pass the pepper, please. This spaghetti is a little under-seasoned."

"You have no way of getting them," Clarence said. "It's an empty threat."

Master Melville dabbed at the corners of his mouth with a napkin. "Fortunately, we have several associates who are willing to do just this kind of work for us. It's quite amazing what people will do for money. All they need is a single word from us."

"You don't have any 'associates,'" Lilly said. "I don't believe it."

"Well, you can always take the risk. If it's worth it to you."

"Don't you dare touch my little brother," she warned.

Mistress lowered her voice so they had to lean forward to hear. "Don't make us have to."

"Ugh!" Lilly stood up. "You disgust me! You're monsters! You don't have hearts, you have rotten toads in your chests. You sleep on a bed of nails. You drink blood. I hate the both of you."

"One more thing," sniffed Mistress, pointing her fork at Lilly. "It's time you earned your keep. Everyone works here, there are no slackers. You *shall* become Napoleon. I'm sure the others can help you to get ready."

Sullivan had never seen anyone look as angry as Lilly did at that moment. And hopeless too, with her small fists clenched at her sides, her nostrils flaring. But all she did was turn and walk away.

"I believe we have chocolate biscuits for dessert," Master Melville said calmly. "I do look forward to our being a happy family again."

❦

Sullivan, Clarence, and Lilly stood on the grass looking down at Napoleon. The contraption certainly looked more than a hundred years old. The ornate lower cabinet, polished oak with handles of brass, was clearly the work of a master carpenter. From it rose the upper body, a wood-and-wire frame clothed in the hand-sewn uniform of a French general—a blue coat with gold epaulettes and a scarlet sash. The face under the boat-shaped hat was carved of wood and had the hollow stare of a ventriloquist's dummy. But the automaton's condition also made it look old, for the wood was banged and scuffed and worn, the costume was faded and threadbare, the face chipped and scratched.

"*Master* Melville," Lilly growled. "Master of what, I'd like to know. How about I make him a master of being punched in the nose?"

"Why not?" Clarence said. "You've already given him one in the eye."

Lilly looked again at Napoleon. "You actually crawled into that dirty pile of junk every night?"

"I fixed the odd rip here and there," Clarence said defensively. "I touched up the face, too."

"Must have taken you all of five minutes. How does it open?"

"There's a hidden latch. I'll show you. You press it like this and then tip the whole figure. It's on a big hinge."

Lilly bent over to see inside the cabinet. "Doesn't look very comfortable, even for someone who can fit in."

"It's not. It's hard on your behind and your back. Your knees, too. And the air gets pretty stale."

"Lovely. And nobody can see you when you're inside? Even when the doors of the cabinet are opened?"

"You have to change position. See, when this door opens, you have to lean forward. But when the door beside it opens, you have to pull up your legs."

"What's this lever? And this bit of wire?"

"I don't know, they never worked."

They closed up Napoleon again. Lilly crouched down and put a finger to its nose. "You know, when I found that handbill in the door the other day, I got really excited. I thought that maybe this time *I* would get to play against Napoleon. I thought he really was an automaton. I thought the key really did wind up springs and gears. Isn't that weird? I mean, there are super-smart computers that can beat world chess champions. Why would anybody be excited about a musty old bunch of clockwork? But I was."

"You're not the only one," Sullivan said. "The audience loves Napoleon. I never really thought about why. Maybe it's the same reason that people like to see Freddy doing magic or me throwing things in the air. They still want to be amazed. Computers are too complicated, nobody understands them. But the stuff we do is different. It takes old-fashioned skill, I guess."

"So are you going to do it?" Clarence asked Lilly. "Operate Napoleon, I mean."

Lilly blew out between her pursed lips, making a sound like a deflating balloon. Then she shook up her own hair with her hand, as if she were trying to shake up her thoughts. "I don't exactly have a choice. I'm not defeated by Tweedledum and Tweedledee, not by a long shot. But I need time to figure out what to do. So for now I'll cooperate and throw them off the scent. Besides, I'm kind of curious just to try it. But I need a few things."

"What things?" Sullivan asked.

"Needle and threads of different colours. Fabric dye. Paint and brushes. Furniture polish. Brass polish. Machine oil. Some small screws and wire. Also some foam cushions to save my butt. And one more thing. A yellow leotard. It'll be easier to fit inside if I'm not in regular clothes."

"Better than underwear," Clarence said. "But why yellow?"

"Because yellow is my favourite colour. Now go," she said, shooing Sullivan away. "Go tell Mr. Moustache."

"Me?"

"You don't actually think *I'm* going to talk to him, do you? If I do, I really will punch him in the nose."

"Fine, I'll do it." Secretly, Sullivan was glad to be of help. After all, he was responsible for her being here.

He wrote the list on the back of an old handbill

and then turned to find Master Melville, but he couldn't see him anywhere. They were staying beside a pick-your-own strawberry field, only it wasn't the growing season so there was just the plowed-over field, an empty shack, a makeshift children's playground with homemade swings and a climber, and an old tree house. It took several moments for Sullivan to realize that Master Melville was actually *up* in the tree house. Master Melville was holding on to the trunk of the tree as if he were afraid that the boards under his feet would give way.

"Master Melville? Why are you up there?"

"Have you never heard of curiosity, my boy?" he asked, careful not to let go of the tree. "This structure must be a hundred years old. I find that interesting. Now, what do you want?"

"Lilly has a list of things that she needs. She wants to fix up Napoleon."

"She does, does she? Not good enough for her, I suppose. Hold on a moment while I come down."

Master Melville half turned as he looked for secure footing. *"Yowzah!"* His foot crashed through a board, but he managed to grab hold of a branch just in time. He extracted his foot and inched himself down the rickety ladder.

At the bottom, Master Melville brushed himself off. "I'm glad to see that I haven't lost all of my youthful vigour. Now, what exactly does that difficult child want?" He took the list from Sullivan's hand. "Hmm. Nothing that sounds too dangerous. I shall go into town. You tell her that I had to go anyway—that I'm not making a special trip for her!"

"Perhaps you'd like to tell her yourself."

"No, no, I've no time."

Master Melville walked quickly away. At that moment, Sullivan realized that the man was more than a little afraid of the girl.

❈

Using the box of supplies, Lilly became so absorbed in restoring Napoleon that she forgot to insult the Melvilles. At meals her mind seemed far away; Sullivan was sure that she was thinking about the next repair. Mistress stopped locking her up at night. Instead, Lilly watched the show from the wings, just as Sullivan had once done.

Whenever he wasn't busy working on his new act, Sullivan volunteered to act as Lilly's assistant. He handed her lengths of thread as she carefully sewed up tears and restored seams. He helped her to mix the fabric dye and then carefully rub it into Napoleon's costume. She set him to work polishing the oak cabinet with slow, circular strokes. Then he began on the brass parts.

"It's the workings inside that are the real challenge," she said while kneeling, hands inside the cabinet. "It's tricky enough to replace parts for the controls that work—like the eye rolling. But I have to figure out what these other things are supposed to do. All the connecting rods and wires are gone. But I've got some ideas. Actually, for this I don't need you any more. In fact, I'd prefer some space. But thanks, you've been a great help."

With that, she dismissed Sullivan. Reluctantly, he wandered away. He'd enjoyed working beside her; in fact, he'd been more content than he had felt in ages.

It took her all the rest of that day to finish. The final touch was putting some cut pieces of foam inside. Then she called the others over.

"What do you think?" Lilly took a step back to admire her handiwork.

"It's amazing," Esmeralda said.

"Transformed," Clarence admitted. "Now I see how shabby it looked before."

"Not bad," was all Frederick said.

Everyone but Sullivan and Lilly wandered away.

"Hey, Dexter," she said. "I keep meaning to thank

you. For trying to save me the night those goons kidnapped me. And look what you got for it. A wallop with a frying pan."

"Don't thank me. It's my fault that you're here in the first place."

"I have no idea what you're talking about."

"I told Mistress your name. She didn't know it and I told her."

"I'm sure she tricked you out of it. You couldn't be devious enough to out-think that black widow spider. You know, as you were waking up after getting conked on the head, you said some pretty funny things."

"Like what?"

"You said that you wanted to visit a pickle farm."

"I didn't!"

"You did. And you said that all the colours in the world were having a party."

"You're totally making that up."

"You also called me Mommy. But I won't tell. Not as long as you give me half of your desserts."

"Okay."

"I'm kidding! Oh shoot, here comes Muddlebrain."

Sullivan saw Master Melville walking towards them, an uneasy smile fixed on his face.

"I hope I'm not intruding."

"You're always intruding," Lilly said.

"Always joking, young Lilly. Now I don't want to rush you, but I did notice what a splendid restoration you've done. When you do join our little show, the workload will become easier for the others. So do just tell me when you're ready—"

"I'm ready now," Lilly cut him off. "Tonight."

"Really? Your enthusiasm is admirable. But perhaps some coaching from Clarence would be wise."

"I don't need coaching. And I'm getting bored standing around and watching everyone else."

Master Melville pulled at his ear. "Tonight it is, then. Sullivan, you're responsible for helping Lilly in and out of the cabinet and getting it on and off the stage. Remember, young lady, play up the drama!"

"I know how to be dramatic," she said and walked away.

Master Melville stood beside Sullivan and watched her go. "An unusual girl. Keep your eye on her, Dexter. I don't mean for my sake. For hers."

Master Melville walked back to the caravan, where Mistress was changing the strings on her banjo-ukulele. He didn't have to tell Sullivan to look out for Lilly; Sullivan felt responsible enough. Besides, Lilly was such an interesting person. Headstrong—that was the term his father would have used. Being headstrong, Gilbert Mintz had said, could get a person into trouble. But maybe it could get a person out of trouble, too.

* 15 *

THE MECHANICAL LAUGH

THEY were set up in the midst of a small group of summer holiday cabins, closed for the season. A large crowd was gathered around the stage—parents with children in their laps, teenagers hanging around the edges, old people sitting on folding chairs. Mistress struck up "The Plowboy Hop" as she strummed, blew, and thumped. Master Melville sprinted onto the stage with a wide grin and a big wave to the "good people of this fair district." He told them what a treat they were in for, flashed a bottle of Hop-Hop Drops, and gave a big buildup to Frederick.

• 151 •

On stage, Frederick's movements had become even more elegant and precise. He was haughtier than ever, too, like some European aristocrat who had somehow ended up in the middle of nowhere. Neither the death of Snit nor the capture of Lilly had put Frederick off his goal of becoming a real artist. Sullivan couldn't help feeling a little jealous of Frederick's improvement.

As his own new routine wasn't ready, there was nothing for him to do now but go on with the old one. Clarence followed with the dogs. Caesar was growing quickly and it was becoming clear that he was going to be a big dog, two or three times bigger than Snoot. But for now he was still a rambunctious puppy. Esmeralda held on to him during most of Clarence's act but she let him dash out onto the stage near the end. Snoot knew how to get Caesar to run around Clarence's legs and do a couple of other things, but even when Caesar didn't cooperate, the audience laughed.

Sullivan went behind the caravan, where he found Lilly standing beside Napoleon. She wore the yellow leotard and it made her look even smaller. She had goosebumps on her arms.

"Okay, I admit it," she said. "I'm freaked out."

"You'll be fine. I know this sounds weird but try to enjoy yourself."

"If you say so," Lilly said weakly. This girl had stood up to the Melvilles, yet the idea of being in front of an audience—even hidden inside Napoleon—was making her tremble all over. Sullivan tipped open the top half and took her hand as she stepped inside.

"Batten down the hatches," she whimpered.

Sullivan brought the top down over Lilly's crouching body. He wheeled the cabinet around to the wings much more easily now that she had cleaned and oiled the wheels. Master Melville was speaking in front of the curtain.

"Our supply of these miraculous drops is limited, and I do suggest you stock up by buying two or even three bottles. But now, ladies and gentlemen, let me present to you a most curious and puzzling artifact, a work of machinery over one hundred years old. It is run by the most simple mechanistic laws of push and pull, rise and fall. It is the creation of an ingenious watchmaker whose name has been lost to time . . ."

Sullivan rapped twice on the side of the cabinet. He heard Lilly's answering thump.

Master Melville cried, "Presenting . . . Napoleon!" and Frederick opened the curtain as Sullivan wheeled the cabinet onto the stage. He almost wished that he could stay but he retreated to the wings. Master

Melville opened the little cabinet doors to show the audience the machinery, swivelled Napoleon around, then set up the chessboard.

Next, he chose a volunteer, a man with a pipe in his mouth and tufts of hair behind his ears. Several people patted the man heartily on the back. Master Melville took the large key out of his waistcoat and made a show of winding up the automaton.

"Are you ready to play, Napoleon?"

Napoleon's arm jerked up and then saluted. A whirring sound came from inside as the arm picked up a pawn and moved it forward. The man moved his own pawn. Napoleon replied without hesitation. After several more moves, the man cried, "Got you!" and captured one of Napoleon's bishops.

Napoleon slowly rotated its head from side to side. Then the machine made its move. The man followed, then Napoleon, then the man again, and all the while Master Melville added his own exciting play-by-play to heighten the drama.

Sullivan could see that the man was slowly surrounding Napoleon's king.

Clarence sidled up to him. "It's been a tight game and Lilly's got herself into a tough spot. Still, nobody can blame her for losing her first—"

Clarence stopped talking. Because Napoleon's

wooden jaw was working up and down and a weird laugh was coming from it.

"How did she do *that*?"

The arm lurched forward, the fingers grasped a pawn and moved it ahead one square.

"That's not much of a move," Sullivan said.

"No, look. She's moved the pawn out of the queen's path. Now she's got him in check. And the pawn is blocking one side. Hold on, the bishop and rook are blocking the other. I think it's actually . . ."

"*Check . . . mate*," the automaton said in a wheezy, mechanical voice.

The crowd roared. The man with the pipe shook his head and then turned and waved at the audience. Sullivan couldn't help smiling. As the curtain closed he rushed to wheel Napoleon out through the wings and around to the back. He felt so anxious to get Lilly out that he couldn't find the hidden latch. At last he touched it and tipped over the upper half.

"Lilly, are you okay?"

Her bangs were plastered to her forehead but otherwise she looked fine. "They liked it, didn't they?"

"You were great. Here, put this towel around your shoulders so you don't catch a chill. The audience loved you."

"Did Napoleon really look like a machine?"

"Completely. You convinced everyone. I think you convinced me."

"I have to admit, it was kind of fun."

Behind her, Sullivan saw Master Melville coming towards them.

"I've only got a moment," he said. "But I must compliment you, young lady. You are a magnificent Napoleon, the best we've ever had."

"I didn't do it for you. I did it for myself."

And at that, Lilly raised her chin and walked away, the towel around her shoulders.

"I don't care who she does it for," Master Melville said to Sullivan. "As long as she does it." Then he turned on his heel and walked back to the stage.

✳ 16 ✳

HIGH SPIRITS

ITH Clarence and the dogs back in the show, and the triumphant return of Napoleon, the applause was getting more enthusiastic every night. So was the demand for Hop-Hop Drops. Every night a line of people waited with their ten-dollar bills in hand, putting Master Melville in a jovial mood.

Along with a better show came at least a semblance of calm, something that none of them had felt for ages. There had been so much upheaval lately that a few days without disruption felt almost like a holiday. They woke up, they made breakfast, they practised or lounged about, they set up the stage, made dinner, prepared, put on the show, sold Hop-Hop Drops, packed up, and slept as the caravan moved on.

As for Lilly, Sullivan noticed a change during her first days as Napoleon. She made a few wisecracks about the Melvilles and still talked about the day she was going to escape. But she stopped suggesting one scheme after another. At night in bed, she was so tired from the exertion of performing that she was the first to fall asleep.

Sullivan thought it might be the right time to bring out his new act. He wasn't feeling especially confident about it, but on the other hand, he probably never would. He had put together a costume of sorts: a ragged pair of too-short pants, a faded shirt, a black vest, scuffed shoes, the bowler hat. He could use a piece of coal, picked up near an old mine, to put some smudges on his face. He didn't think more practice would help. He had to put the act on stage and see what worked and what didn't.

So far he hadn't shown it to anyone, not even Clarence. But he was going to need the others as bit players in the drama. So he approached everyone in turn—Clarence, Esmeralda, Lilly, Frederick, and even Master Melville—and showed them what to do. He asked Mistress if she would play only her violin and, while she gave him a dark look, she didn't say no. And then, just before showtime, he appeared in his new getup, face smudged with coal, bowler hat set back on his head. Nobody teased Sullivan; they knew what a scary moment this was. All of them stood in the wings to watch and to be ready for their own parts.

As soon as the curtain opened, Mistress put her bow to the strings. Sullivan didn't know the tune she was playing, but it was slow and melancholy, and it made it easier for him to look hungry and sad as he stood with his hands in his pockets. A man (played by Master Melville) passed by and Sullivan held out his hand for a little change, but the man just put his handkerchief to his nose as if to ward off a bad smell. Next, a girl in a bonnet (Lilly) and a boy in knickers (Clarence) strolled by, only to laugh at him as they passed.

Sullivan tried to look even more dejected. A tough-looking young man with a cap pulled over his eyes (Frederick) sauntered by with a girl (Esmeralda) on his arm. Suddenly the young man snatched the bowler hat from Sullivan's head. Sullivan lunged for it but the young man pulled away. He pranced about, teasing, holding it up high.

The audience watched in absolute silence. Was that good or bad? The young man carelessly tossed the hat in the air and ran from the stage. Sullivan scrambled for it (Frederick's throw had been off), grabbed it with his fingertips, and rolled it up his arm, around his neck, and down the other arm. He tossed it up into the air where it turned over and over before he caught it on the toe of his upraised foot. He kicked it into the air and caught it in his hands.

All this time the girl, played by Esmeralda, had been watching. Delighted, she dropped a few coins into the upturned hat. Sullivan made a puzzled face and then, picking up the coins, looked at them in amazement.

The crowd clapped with pleasure.

The rest of the act was too repetitive, he decided. He juggled balls and someone put coins in his hat. He juggled torches, he got more coins. Even as he performed, he saw how changes might be made. When he bowed and hurried off stage as the curtain closed, he got a hug from Esmeralda, a slap on the back from Clarence, and even a "Good job" from Frederick.

Lilly waited for him beside Napoleon. "Pretty sweet act. Too bad I missed the end."

"You didn't miss that much. It needs work."

She raised her hand and with a finger rubbed some coal dust from his cheek. "You're a surprising one, that's for sure. Now you'd better get me out there."

She stepped into the cabinet and slunk down. Even as he closed the lid, he felt the touch of her hand on his cheek.

❋

All the rest of that night, Lilly was very much on Sullivan's mind. She might have been small but she was also noisy, abrupt, bossy, difficult, funny, brave, and smart. She was a messy eater, sometimes she laughed like a hyena, and every so often she liked to punch somebody in the arm just for fun. She wasn't beautiful—not Esmeralda-beautiful, at least—but she had the most wonderful face and big eyes and funny smile. Esmeralda, he saw now, was meant to be a wonderful friend but not more than that. She had been so nice to him, it wasn't surprising that he had mistaken his gratitude for something else. And Esmeralda and Frederick—well, they seemed to need each other. But these new feelings he had for Lilly were different from anything he'd known before. All he wanted now was more days of this calm, so that he might have another moment like that with her. So that he might find out how she felt. If only nothing happened to ruin it.

And then came dinner.

With the rise in sales of Hop-Hop Drops, their meals had improved considerably. That night Master Melville himself had organized the cooking—Mediterranean fish soup followed by a spicy couscous. They sat near the spreading branches of an enormous oak tree in which a flock of small birds argued. Nearby, Caesar shook a stick, dropped it, growled, and shook it again while Snoot watched placidly. Everyone was enjoying the food when Master Melville raised his glass of wine.

"I propose a toast," he announced.

"Must you?" Mistress said.

"Yes, my sweet ear of corn, I must. I am in high spirits and cannot help myself. The show, as you all know, is going splendidly. And it is thanks to all your extraordinary talents. We were a fine group before, most certainly, but it is the addition of our Lilly here that has brought us closer to the pinnacle of artistic heights."

Master Melville drank his wine to the last drop, tipping back his head. He straightened again, a look of immense satisfaction on his face, but then registered surprise at the sight of Lilly standing up.

"How dare you?" Lilly said, her voice barely controlled. "How dare you say *our Lilly*? Do you think that I *belong* to you? Do you think that, just because I've agreed to perform, I accept being here? Do you think I see you as some kindly uncle? Or that I see Catwoman over there as our mother hen?"

"Now, child . . ." Master Melville interjected.

"I'm talking, not you. You don't fool me for a second. Never, ever call me *our Lilly* again. Do you hear me?"

And at that Lilly picked up the pot of fish soup, or what was left of it, and tossed it—pot and all—at Master Melville. He ducked. The pot missed him, but not most of the soup. Then she stomped away.

Sullivan and the rest of them sat there as if frozen. Master Melville picked a shrimp off his shoulder.

"That young woman does like a grand exit," he sighed.

But Sullivan knew. The calm was over.

❈

That night in bed, as the caravan moved on, Sullivan could just *feel* Lilly seething in the dark. He could also hear her—smacking her pillow with her hand, huffing angrily to herself.

Clarence sighed loudly. "Come on already, Lilly. Say something before you burst."

"What is there to say? Scream maybe. I don't have words for how I feel."

"You like to be so dramatic," Frederick said. "He was only giving you a compliment."

"Don't, Freddy," Esmeralda chimed in. "You'll just upset her more."

Sullivan said, "I think you would feel better if we were doing something about being here."

"I know what I'd like to do. I'd like to take that frying pan—"

"That's not exactly what I meant. Maybe we need another approach to our situation."

"Like what?" Esmeralda asked.

"Like finding out what the Melvilles are doing. I mean, they can't be running this medicine show just because they love wearing old-fashioned clothes and sleeping in a different place every night. There's got to be some other reason."

"Sure," Clarence said. "I've thought about that too. But I can't think of any."

"Have you noticed Monty snooping around every place that we stop? What's he looking for?"

"We've all noticed that," Frederick said. "I always figured he was just hunting for stuff. You know, things that people have thrown away or lost."

"But he never brings anything back."

"There must be some way of finding out." Lilly didn't sound mad now; she sounded intrigued. "Some information somewhere. The only place that we don't get to see is the Melvilles' side of the caravan. Maybe there's a clue in there. Has anybody ever been inside?"

"Only Dexter," Frederick said. "When he gave them your name."

"Thanks a lot, Freddy."

"It wasn't your fault. But did you see anything that might be a clue? Anything at all?" Lilly asked.

"To be honest, I've tried not to think about it."

"Try now," Clarence said. "Imagine you're in the Melvilles' quarters. Tell us what you see."

Sullivan closed his eyes. He took a deep breath and let it out slowly. "Okay. I'm sitting on this sofa that's covered in leather. There's another one right across. That's where the Black Death is sitting. Between us on the right is an end table."

"What's on the table?" Esmeralda asked.

"Two mugs and the drink she gave me."

"There must be something else in the room," Frederick said impatiently.

"A rug. A lamp hanging from the ceiling. A little shelf built into the wall. With a few books on it."

"What books?" Clarence asked.

"I don't know. Old books."

"Maybe one of them is a false book," Lilly said. "You know, with the pages cut out in the middle so you can hide things in it."

"Maybe," Sullivan said doubtfully. "They weren't very thick."

"In other words, nothing of interest." Frederick yawned. "Can we go to sleep now?"

Sullivan tried to picture the shelf more clearly. There was something else there, he was sure of it.

"Also an album," he remembered suddenly.

"An album?" Lilly asked. "Like an old record album?"

"No, like a photograph album. Or maybe a scrapbook. Something like that. It had a black cover and it was taller than the other books. It had a little label on the spine.

"What did the label say?" Lilly asked.

"I don't remember."

"Try," Clarence urged. "Try harder."

Caesar whimpered. Sullivan squeezed shut his eyes. He tried to go back to that place he didn't want to go to. He could taste the sweet, heady drink that Mistress had given him. He could see the lamp sending its flickering light over the walls. The label was faded and the writing on it had fancy lettering.

"History of something," Sullivan said.

"Keep trying," Lilly urged.

"Some letters. They were almost all the same, a lot of *M*s. With periods after each letter, like they stood for something. *M.M.M.*—three of them. And some other letter. *P*? *E*? *B*? It's no good, I can't remember."

"You did great," Esmeralda said. "*History of M.M.M.* with one other letter."

"An *S*!" Clarence cried. "It *has* to be an *S*. Because *M.M.M.S.* would stand for Master Melville's Medicine Show."

"I think you're right. It was an *S*."

"Brilliant!" Lilly said. "I could kiss you, Dexter."

Sullivan blushed in the dark. Lilly had just made his painful remembering worthwhile. But the moment was broken by Frederick.

"I hate to rain on your parade but it doesn't make sense. Why would this show have a history? It's probably just Monty's diary. 'Sold twenty bottles. Good show tonight.' Useless stuff like that."

"We won't know until we see it," Lilly said. "I think it's our best chance to learn something. I'm going to get on the other side of that wall, one way or another. Then we'll find out what's in that album."

Sullivan looked down the caravan towards Lilly, even though he couldn't see anything in the dark. "No, you're not," he said with a firmness he didn't completely feel. "I'm the one who knows where it is. I'm the one who has to go in."

* 17 *

AMAZING AND STUPENDOUS

$\mathcal{S}$OMEONE walking into the kitchen of the Stardust Home for Old People might have thought that a box of plumbing supplies—pipes and connectors and drain fittings—had been accidentally dumped onto the floor. In fact, they had all come from underneath the double sink, where Gilbert was now crouched with a wrench in his hand.

"Ow! I just banged my head! There's no room under here."

At the end of the counter there was another mess, this one of papers. Loretta stood there, picking up one sheet and then another. "It isn't just the mortgage," she said. "It's the heating. Electricity. Three repair bills."

"I know there are three repair bills," Gilbert said. "That's why I'm trying to fix the sink myself."

"Are you sure you know what you're doing?"

"No, I'm not sure at all."

"Dinner has to get started in an hour."

"Loretta, you're really not helping. Can you possibly find something else to do?"

"All right. I'll go to the library for an hour."

"Excellent idea."

Loretta put on her coat and scarf and gloves and rode her bicycle into town. The bicycle didn't belong to her but to one of the residents, Eliot McReady, who used it to ride around the block for exercise. Loretta was always worried that he would fall or crash into something, but she knew that riding was the highlight of his day. He had kindly offered the use of it to Loretta so that she wouldn't have to keep walking into town to go to the library. She took it from the porch of the Stardust Home and began to ride against a very chilly wind.

The truth was that Loretta didn't feel very optimistic. She had begun her reading of old newspapers with great enthusiasm, but many hours of fruitless searching had begun to make her feel as if she was looking for a needle in a haystack—if there was a needle in there at all. Perhaps there were no more articles about the original medicine show. And even if there were, what were the chances of her finding one?

But since she had no better idea, Loretta settled herself in front of the library computer once more. The kind librarian made her another cup of tea and she searched through the pages of the *Norfolk County Times*, the *Pontenesca Digest*, and the *Remington Record*. She was on her third cup of tea and her eyes were beginning to tear from the strain when a headline in the *Fenton's Corners Informer* caught her attention.

Happiness in a Bottle?
Medicine Show Offers Youthful Entertainment

Loretta stared at the screen. She moved her face closer and read the words again.

"I need to print this out!"

The librarian helped her to make several copies. Then she sprinted out of the building and got onto the bicycle. Her hands were shaking so badly that she almost rode into a lamppost. She reached the Stardust Home, carried the bicycle onto the porch, and rushed to the kitchen.

"Is your husband a genius or what?" Gilbert said

with a grin. "Got that sink working perfectly. Now I'm making veal parmigiana. Only we can't afford veal so it's chicken. Just as good, in my opinion. Hey, are you okay, Loretta? You look kind of pale."

"Read this," Loretta said and thrust a copy at him. His hands were messy with egg and bread crumbs so she held it up for him.

Gilbert's eyebrows shot up. "This is amazing! This is stupendous. Loretta, you found it! This is the best chance we've had."

"We have to tell Manny and Jinny," Loretta said. "They phoned a few days ago, when they were leaving the Samartinos'. That means they should phone again any time."

At that moment the telephone rang. They both turned and looked as it rang again. Loretta snatched up the receiver.

"Manny? I'm so glad it's you. Listen carefully. You have to go to Fenton's Corners. . . . That's right. The original medicine show played there a hundred years ago this Saturday. That's in three days. You have to be there waiting for them. And we're going to come, too. I think this is it, Manny. We're going to get Sullivan back!"

Manny put Jinny on the telephone and Loretta had to explain all over again. Then she had to read the old newspaper article to them. The article described the show and mentioned the reward for anyone who could prove that the magical drops didn't work. Gilbert spoke to them, too, and then they hung up. Loretta hugged Gilbert. And then he went back to cooking and she began to set the table, because no matter how excited they were, forty-seven old people still need their dinner.

When the table was set and all the residents in their seats, Loretta began to serve. The front doorbell rang. "I don't have time!" she cried, but she hurried to the door anyway. There in the doorway stood Norval Simick and Samuel Patinsky.

"We wanted to show you the buttons we made," Norval said.

Samuel gave her a button.

"I love it!" Loretta pinned it to her shirt. "Now you can help serve and stay for dinner, if you like. Just call your parents first."

The boys made their calls and joined Loretta in serving. Norval found himself carrying several dinner plates on a very large tray—it wobbled for a moment, and they all held their breath, but he managed to get his balance. When everyone was served, the boys sat down with the Mintzes.

"Actually, this is my second dinner," Samuel said. "But I was still hungry."

Gilbert said, "We've got news, boys. We know where Sullivan is going to be on Saturday."

"You do?" Norval's eyes widened. "Fantastic! Can we come?"

"I don't think so. It might be dangerous. But you could drop in here and lend a hand while we're away. That would be a huge help."

"Can we eat dinner while we're here?" Samuel asked, forking up some mashed potatoes.

* 18 *

A HUMDINGER

THE performers woke up to find that a small and battered canvas tent had been erected behind the caravan.

Lilly looked at the tent as she helped to prepare breakfast. On the side were some faded words: *Mandoni's Miniature Circus. Half the Size, Twice the Fun.* "What exactly goes on in there?" she asked. "Some freaky sideshow? A lamb with two heads, or a mermaid in a bottle?"

"It's brewing and bottling day. Monty's in the tent

making more Hop-Hop Drops," Sullivan explained. "We must be getting low."

"Terrific. That means Droopy Whiskers will be occupied. This is your chance to sneak into the caravan and get a look at the album."

"Right . . . I mean, great!" Sullivan tried to sound sincere.

Master Melville didn't come out of the tent for breakfast. Sullivan could hear curses and pots clanging and steam hissing. Smoke rose from a flap at the top of the tent. He'd moved the table they usually used into the tent, so they had to eat on their laps—muffins with butter and jam and cups of tea. But Sullivan had no appetite, his courage having already vanished.

After cleanup, Lilly stationed Esmeralda and Clarence at strategic lookout points to keep an eye on the tent, while Mistress Melville sat on a tree stump practising a new tune on her banjo-ukulele.

When Sullivan got the all-clear, he crept to the front of the caravan, pulled himself up, and squeezed between the riders' seats to the small door behind. He opened the door, ducked in, and shut it again.

It was pitch-black inside. He struck a match and lit a candle. He saw the two leather sofas, the end table, the shelf of books.

The album was gone.

Not believing his eyes, he took out all the books and then felt along the shelf. He put the books back and looked on the sofas, the end table, checked the floor. He saw a trunk pushed into the corner that he had somehow missed before, but there were only clothes inside.

"Damn and tarnation! I've burned myself!"

It was Master Melville. It sounded as if he had suddenly burst from the tent. The others hadn't had a chance to warn him. Keeping still, Sullivan could hear Lilly say something about the first-aid kit. Mistress called him a clumsy oaf.

"Dexter? Where's Dexter?" Master Melville called. "I need that boy's help."

Without a wasted motion, Sullivan snuffed out his candle, opened the door, and hopped down from the caravan. He came around the side with his hands in his pockets.

"Did somebody call me?"

Master Melville was letting Lilly wrap gauze around one of his fingers. "There you are. There isn't a moment to lose. If everything isn't timed perfectly, the whole batch will be lost. Come and help me. Into the tent! Don't dawdle, boy!"

Master Melville shooed Lilly away. He opened the tent flap and motioned for Sullivan to hurry.

Sullivan ducked under the flap. He was hit by a blast of humid air and a mix of strange, potent smells. Before him, sitting over a fire, stood the apparatus that was usually stored on top of the caravan—a double boiler with a brass tube that curled round and round and went into a metal bucket. From the bucket rose a glass tube. A purplish liquid rose up it in defiance of gravity before dripping through a series of cloth filters suspended in a wooden frame. From there the liquid collected into a funnel and ran through some more tubing to the bottling station.

But the glass bottle was overflowing, the liquid pouring onto the ground.

"Quick, boy! We're losing the stuff. Replace the bottle and put a cork into the full one. And keep replacing them. Look alive, now."

Sullivan did as he was told. There was a stool for him to sit on, a large stack of empty bottles, a bowl of corks, and a row of filled bottles. He snatched the bottle away, put an empty one in its place, put a cork in the first, and lined it up. He had just enough time to switch the next bottle before it overflowed. Meanwhile, Master Melville danced around the apparatus, turning a lever here, checking the temperature there, feeding the fire, tapping, scooping, stirring.

"I know what you're thinking, Dexter," Master Melville said as he tapped the glass tube. "It takes lightning reflexes and an exact sense of timing. But I can't do it with a bandage on my finger. Your efforts are saving the day."

Sullivan pulled away another full bottle, replacing it with an empty one. He switched and corked and looked up to see Master Melville leaning down to look at a large book propped up on a chair. Only it wasn't a book, it was the album! No wonder he hadn't been able to find it; the recipe for Hop-Hop Drops was inside.

"We need a touch more camphor."

"That must be a pretty old recipe," Sullivan ventured, trying to sound casual.

"Old indeed. And you know how I got it? By chance, sheer chance. Yes, this old album contains many secrets, dear boy, many secrets. Let me tell you something they don't teach in school. The only things really worth learning are what nobody else knows. Watch it, that bottle's about to overflow!"

Sullivan shifted his attention back to the task. "It's pretty amazing," he said. "Drops that actually make people happy. I wonder how it works."

"Ah, now that's a tricky question to answer, Dexter.

One that I've pondered myself. The recipe itself doesn't say. And the ingredients? Obtainable in any good grocery store. This is the way that I think about it. Have you ever noticed how some audiences appreciate your juggling more than others? Even when your performance is of the same quality?"

"Sure."

"And why is that, do you think?"

"Well, if it's not because of me, then it's because of them."

"Exactly. For you see, in any performance, there is one special ingredient. It's the audience. It's the one thing that can't be fully controlled. Without the audience, you're just a boy throwing objects into the air. With an audience, you're a performer.

"I believe that Hop-Hop Drops work the same way. To anyone who doesn't know anything about it, it's just a funny-coloured liquid that doesn't taste very good. But to somebody else—somebody who has heard me extoll its extraordinary properties, somebody who is willing to pay ten dollars of his hard-earned money— it is a powerful and even miraculous medicine. And then it works. And if it works, is it not real medicine? Watch that bottle, Dexter!"

Sullivan switched bottles. "So it's all in their heads?"

"Of course not, dear boy. For it's in my head, too!

Now tell me something. I'd like to offer you a small token of appreciation for assisting me today. What would you like? Don't be unrealistic, though."

Sullivan thought quickly. "How about you make your special fajitas for dinner? Everyone likes them."

"Now that's an excellent suggestion. And of course it gives me an opportunity to head into town for supplies and spread the word about tonight's show. You're a very reasonable boy, Dexter."

But Sullivan wasn't trying to be reasonable; he was trying to get Melville out of the way.

❋

When Master Melville went into town, he did not want to be recognized as the man from the medicine show. "No need to attract the attention of the local constabulary, the town council, or the parent-teacher association, for that matter." He wore his "disguise"—a pair of overalls, a checked shirt, and a battered straw hat.

"You look like an actor playing a farmer in a very bad play," Mistress said.

"My dear," answered Master Melville from his perch on the back of Soggy Biscuit, "I shall blend in. I shall be one of the people." Then he gave the horse a kick with his heels and trotted off.

Master Melville enjoyed these excursions into town. He could shuck off his responsibilities, even the need to placate his dearest Eudora. Going to town was a holiday. On Main Street he would saunter past the shop windows. He would discuss local events with the old-timers lining the bench in front of the local diner. He would tell outlandish stories while getting his moustache trimmed in the barber shop. Along the way he would mention hearing about a show to be put on that very night, an old-fashioned entertainment that was sure to be a "doozy."

On this day, Master Melville set back his hat and walked Soggy Biscuit past the *Welcome* sign for Fenton's Corners. There wasn't much that distinguished the place from any other small town: a bank, a restaurant, two grocery stores, a hotel that had known more prosperous times. He tied Soggy Biscuit's reins to a lamppost and began to walk, tipping his hat to a lady with a baby carriage. He remarked to a man leaning against the bank that it was very fine weather for this time of year. He took a good long look at the two grocery stores before going into the one on the left because he could see a gumball machine through the window.

If he had chosen the other grocery store, all that followed would have been different for Sullivan and his fellow performers. But such is the nature of chance, accident, or fate. Master Melville walked into Pembleton's Fresh Produce whistling "Under the Chicken Tree," bought himself a nickel gumball, and picked up a basket. He found the ingredients he needed, along with a box of double-chocolate cookies, and headed for the cash register.

A stout man in a doorman's uniform and cap was already there, buying himself a can of root beer.

"Mighty pretty town you have here," Master Melville said genially.

"It'll do, I suppose," said the silver-haired Mr. Pembleton behind the counter.

"Hasn't changed much in thirty years," said the man in the uniform.

"As we farmers like to say, the old ways are the good ways." Master Melville smiled at his own piece of folk wisdom.

"Personally, I don't mind something new now and then," said Mr. Pembleton. "Like to get one of those big screens for the home."

"That might do for some," Master Melville said, "but I prefer live entertainment. In fact, I hear there's going to be a show tonight by the covered bridge. Starting at dusk. Magicians and fire-tossers and I don't know what else, but it's supposed to be a humdinger. Suitable for the little ones."

"That's a funny thing," said the man in the uniform. "I work over at the hotel and a man and a girl came in today asking about just such a show."

Master Melville's voice became very quiet. "Is that so? About when?"

"Been here since about noon. Seems they're looking for a boy. A runaway, I suppose. Name of Sullivan."

"But of course you didn't know anything about the show, so you couldn't tell them."

"Oh, they knew about it already. Even knew where it was going to be."

Master Melville put down the basket and headed for the door.

"Hey," cried Mr. Pembleton, "don't you want your groceries?"

"Not hungry!" called Master Melville. He bolted out the door, spat the gumball into the street, and ran in his odd, hop-step fashion towards Soggy Biscuit.

Although Sullivan had asked for a special dinner, he didn't actually see Master Melville heading off to shop in town because he was helping Clarence wash the dogs. Assisting with the Hop-Hop Drops had been tiring and he would have preferred doing nothing for a while, but when Clarence asked him, he didn't want to say no.

He was trying to dry Snoot when Lilly ran up to them.

"Come on, we've got to take this chance!"

"What chance? Oh yuck!" Clarence grimaced as Caesar licked him across the mouth.

"Master Smellville just went to town. And the evil stepmother is sitting over there, painting her nails black. The album must be back inside. Now's your chance, Dexter."

Sullivan looked around warily. "I don't see how we can distract Mistress again."

"We don't have to. I've got a plan all worked out." And then, in a voice loud enough for Mistress to hear, she said, "It's disgraceful, Dexter! Just look at your hair. Are you trying to be a hippie? I'm giving you a haircut this instant."

Without looking up, Mistress said, "Cut off his nose while you're at it."

Lilly called, "Esmeralda! Bring my things out, please." And within two seconds, Esmeralda was walking towards them, holding a chair, a white sheet, a pair of scissors, and a comb.

Lilly instructed her to put down the chair and then told Sullivan to sit on it. He obeyed, and she put her hands on his shoulders to turn him so that he faced away from Mistress. Then she draped the sheet around him.

"Don't worry." She stood behind the chair, making sure to block Mistress's view. With the comb she drew up a bit of hair and snipped it. "Shoot, that was a bit crooked."

"Is this really necessary?"

"Stop moving or I might stab you."

Sullivan noticed Frederick and Clarence coming around from the caravan. Lilly must have told them her plan because they were both making an obvious effort to look casual. They were carrying the "Haunted House" from Frederick's magic act, several flat boards cut and painted to take on the shape of a house when they were unfolded. In his act, Frederick would make it into a house from which would emerge the figure of a ghost. Now he held one end and Clarence the other as they came towards the chair.

"What are you two doing?" Lilly said in an unnaturally loud voice, obviously wanting to make sure that Mistress could hear.

"I need to touch up the paint," Frederick said.

"I'm helping!" chimed in Clarence.

They moved right up beside Lilly.

"Quick," Lilly hissed at Sullivan. "Get behind the house and crouch down."

"What?"

"Just do it!"

Sullivan left the sheet on the chair and slipped behind the house. To his surprise, he heard Lilly continue to snip away with the scissors. "You'll see, Dexter," she said, also in a loud voice. "This is going to be your best haircut ever."

"Keep it down over there!" Mistress called with annoyance.

"Sorry!"

"Okay," Frederick whispered. "You need to move along as we do. And keep low. The boards will hide you."

Before Sullivan could respond, Frederick and Clarence began moving again, the house between them. It was hard to walk while crouched over and Sullivan just managed to keep up. He could still hear the scissors going. Suddenly he understood. Lilly was blocking the view of the Black Death, who couldn't see that Sullivan was no longer on the chair. If she looked up she would still see Lilly snipping away while Frederick and Clarence walked by with the boards.

They walked to the other side of the caravan. "You can stand up, now," Clarence whispered. "The Black Death can't see you here."

Sullivan stood up. "Pretty clever."

"An old magician's trick," Frederick said.

"You'd better hurry, Dex."

Without waiting another moment, Sullivan pulled himself onto the caravan, trying not to make the boards squeak. He opened the small door, went in, and closed it again.

Just as before, he lit the candle, but this time he saw that the album was back on the shelf. He sat on the sofa, pulled it into his lap, and turned over several pages.

How disappointing. It was just an old scrapbook full of yellowed newspaper clippings and handbills and faded photographs. Master Melville hadn't written in it at all. It wasn't about *their* medicine show; it was about some show from a long time ago. In the photographs the men wore stovepipe hats and high collars, and the women wore long dresses and buttoned-up little jackets and had their hair pinned up.

But something didn't make sense. Here was an article about a medicine show run by someone named Montague Melchior Melville along with his wife, Eudora. And here was a faded photograph of a caravan that looked just like their own caravan. It was in front of a feed supply store and there was a row of horses tied up beside it. The names were the same, the caravan looked the same, but the newspapers were from a hundred years ago.

He read one article, then another. His eyes opened

wide as the pieces began to fit together. Could this really mean what he thought it did?

Sullivan was looking at a crumbling old map when he heard the sound of hoofbeats. Master Melville must have returned on Soggy Biscuit. As he closed the album, he heard Master Melville shouting.

"Eudora? *Eudora!* We have a problem, my dear, a very big problem!"

Sullivan's heart jumped. He put the album back on the shelf and snuffed out the candle. The small door flew open, and for a terrifying moment, Sullivan thought the Black Death had found him. But no, it was Lilly, pulling him by the arm. They climbed down from the caravan and hurried to the other side.

"This could be trouble, very big trouble, Eudora!"

"I wish you would be quiet for a moment and let me think."

The Melvilles were standing close together. Sullivan couldn't imagine what was going on with them but he could see that they were concerned. Master Melville nodded, but it was Mistress who spoke to them.

"Load everything back up and then get into the caravan! Right now! All of you!" She turned to her husband. "Lock them in. We've got some tricky work to do."

Sullivan and the others packed everything away,

with the help of Master Melville and even Mistress. Then they filed into the back and heard the lock click shut. They sat on their bunks in the dark, expecting to feel the wheels start to move. Instead, they heard Soggy Biscuit galloping away.

"What in the world is going on?" Clarence asked.

19

STRANGERS IN NEED

$\mathcal{T}$O get to Fenton's Corners, Manny and Jinny had to take a train, a bus, and then hitch a ride with a farmer hauling a load of sheep manure. The farmer had let them off at the far end of Main Street and they had walked on with their packs on their backs. If Loretta Mintz's theory was correct, then this new, copycat medicine show was going to perform just outside of Fenton's Corners that very night. Either that, or they had travelled three days for nothing.

They walked along Main Street until they came to the Grand Hotel. The building's façade butted right up against the sidewalk, four storeys of pale-yellow brick. The front window had once been decorated with the word *Saloon* in dark-red paint, but the letters were chipped and faded. There was a cast-iron lamp on one side of the door but its mate on the other side was missing.

"I think it should be called the Not-Very-Grand Hotel," Jinny said. "It looks like a dump."

"Sure, it's seen better days," Manny answered. "But once upon a time silent-movie stars used to stay here."

"You're pulling the wool over my nose."

After checking in, they rode the creaking elevator up to the fourth floor. Their room was spare but clean, with twin beds and a window looking out behind the hotel. It had what Manny called "the two essentials"— clean sheets and hot water.

They spent the late afternoon relaxing to ballroom dance music on the radio, then ate an early dinner in the town's only restaurant. Back in their room, they took turns soaking in the claw-foot bathtub before getting dressed again.

"Wouldn't hurt us to have a little rest." Manny yawned and stretched out on the bed.

"Is everybody really coming soon?" Jinny said drowsily from her own bed.

"They sure are. Ought to be here in another hour."

Jinny smiled to herself and closed her eyes. Manny looked over and saw that she was already asleep.

Gilbert and Loretta were indeed on their way. So were the Samartinos, whose son Matthew had disappeared with his dogs, and the parents of the red-haired girl, Louise. The only person who had refused to come was the uncle of the older boy, the one who had been good at magic. They were all going to meet in the hotel lobby so they could get organized.

The plan was to arrive at the show in ones and twos, so as not to alert the kidnappers to their presence. At a signal from Manny, they would rush forward, grab hold of their children, and refuse to let them go. With the audience as witnesses, he didn't think that the kidnappers would try to fight them. More likely, they would attempt to flee.

Manny hoped that they could detain the kidnappers, but the first priority was to rescue the kids. Eighty-one years of experience was worth something, and he also knew that plans didn't always go as expected. Anything might happen. Thinking about all the possibilities, Manny, too, fell asleep. His mouth fell open and every so often a snore would fill the room.

The snoring eventually woke Jinny, who got up and sat in front of the old mirror to put her hair in a ponytail. A ponytail meant that a person was ready for action.

A knock sounded on the door.

Jinny went over to Manny's bed and shook him by the shoulder. "Manny? There's somebody at the door."

"What? What's that?"

Manny sat up, swinging his thin legs over the edge of the bed. The knock became more insistent.

"You didn't order room service?" he asked Jinny.

"I didn't even know that the room needed service."

He got up with a wince. Then he opened the door to a couple whose appearance struck him as unusual. The woman, tall and attractive, wore an enormous feathered hat, a fur stole, and a tight-fitting dress covered in shimmering beads. The man had a narrow face with a moustache and pointed beard. He wore a large-brimmed fedora and a white suit with pale-blue stripes.

"May I help you?"

"We truly hope so," said the man, who had a strong accent. It sounded like "*Vee truly hoop zo.*"

"Please come in."

Manny closed the door behind them. The man said, "We are strangers in need. You see, we are searching with desperate feeling for our lost children."

"Children? More than one?"

"Three," said the woman, fluttering her eyelashes at Manny. "Triplets. Such wonderful, talented children.

They learned to form a human pyramid when they were only six months old. But our darling boys have disappeared." The woman held a polka-dot handkerchief to her nose and blew noisily.

"That's terrible," Manny commiserated. "We may know who took them. You see, we're looking for a child of our own."

"So we heard at the front desk," said the man. "Your boy likes to juggle. This is the reason for us to be here. Let me give you my card, to prove we are legitimate people. Our name is Horfmutter. If you could help us to get our children back, there would be much happiness raining down on our heads."

"We have a plan to do just that," Manny said, looking at the card. The name on it was written three times.

~~The Hoorfffmudders~~
~~The Huurvmothers~~
The Horfmutters

Manny slipped the card into his pocket. "We're going to liberate the children."

"That is capital! We certainly wish to help bring these miscreants to justice. A half hour, you say? Then we must get ready. We will find a rope, or a baseball hitter, perhaps a pointy umbrella. We must be armed. Then we will join your posse."

"You will be most welcome."

"Again, we thank you. So we will make a stand at Fenton's Corners."

"Husband," said the wife sharply. "We keep these good people too long."

"Of course."

The Horfmutters bowed many times over as they backed out of the room. Manny closed the door.

"Eccentric people, I must say. And the poor fellow can hardly spell his own name. But they are suffering the same as us. Now, how shall we pass the time until everyone else arrives? We need something to calm our nerves. Shall we continue the world's longest-running game of gin rummy?"

"Okay," Jinny said and went to get the cards from her backpack. She sat down on Manny's bed and began to shuffle them by breaking the cards up into little heaps and then piling them together. Something was bothering her about the Horfmutters, but she didn't know what. They looked familiar and yet she couldn't say why. She gave the cards to Manny, who dealt them out.

"What's the score?" he said.

"I'm winning by three thousand points . . . Manny?"

"Yes, Jinny?"

"When Sullivan comes home, is he still going to be Sullivan?"

"Do you mean, will he have changed?"

"I guess that's what I mean."

"Well, he's gone through a lot. He's lived without us. He's had to learn to survive. He's been performing in front of audiences. No doubt he's grown up a good deal. I expect that he won't be exactly the same as we remember him. But he'll still be your big brother."

"I hope so."

She put down three cards.

"Manny, those people, the Horsefeathers."

"Horfmutters."

"They knew that Sullivan liked to juggle."

"That's right." Manny began to pick up cards.

"I heard you talking to the man at the desk. You never told him that Sullivan liked to juggle."

He held a card in mid-air. "You're right. I never did tell him. That's a bit peculiar. You don't suppose—"

"Manny, I smell something funny."

The old man sniffed the air. "My sense of smell isn't what it used to be. What do you smell?"

"Marshmallows."

"That's nice."

"*Burning* marshmallows."

Manny sniffed again. "Yes, now I smell it. Someone must be having a barbecue."

Jinny dropped her cards. She stood up and pointed. "I see smoke!"

Manny saw the fear in Jinny's face. He followed her gaze to the bottom of the door that led to the hallway. Wisps of smoke curled from underneath. He jumped up, hurried to the door, and grabbed the knob.

The door wouldn't open.

"Jinny, help me to push. Hard!"

They threw themselves at the door but it didn't budge. Jinny started to kick it.

"That won't help. Don't be afraid. We'll go to the window and use the back fire escape."

The smoke made Jinny cough. She clung to Manny as they moved to the window. On the sill was a vase of dried flowers. He knocked it off in his hurry to turn the latch and haul the window up. Together they put their heads out and looked down. They could see flames shooting up from the windows below. Where was the fire escape? Then Manny saw it—dismantled and lying on the ground below.

"We can't get out!" Jinny cried. "We're going to burn up!"

A popping sound from below sent a huge flame scorching upwards. Manny grabbed Jinny and pulled her back inside as it roared past.

✻ 20 ✻

THE AWFUL TRUTH

BEING in a small space—if not by choice, then at least by habit—can be tolerable. But being locked up unexpectedly, deprived of light and freedom, is a different thing altogether. All the performers were used to being in the caravan at night, but being forced inside during the day made them feel as restless as animals in a cage.

Sullivan could hear Clarence get up from his bunk and suddenly bang his fists on the door. The dogs growled and whined at his feet.

"Let us out of here! Somebody! Let us out!"

• 199 •

"There's nobody around to hear you," Frederick said. "You're wasting your breath. Why don't you just relax? Maybe Melville needs to get a tooth pulled. It could be a million things. Personally, I don't mind having a break."

"You're pretty quiet, Lilly," Esmeralda said. "Are you okay?"

"I'm feeling a bit claustrophobic, to tell you the truth. Like I can't breathe. And I don't like the dark."

"*You're* afraid of the dark?" Frederick sounded as if he didn't believe her.

"Is there some reason I can't be?"

"No, I'm just surprised. You act so tough."

"At home I still use a night light."

"Dexter, why don't you go and sit with Lilly," Esmeralda suggested.

"Sure."

Good old Esmeralda, thought Sullivan. She picked up everything. He went over and sat on the bunk. After hesitating a moment, he reached out. She grasped his hand.

"Hey," Clarence said. "With everything going on, we forgot to ask Dexter what he saw in the Melvilles' quarters. Did you find the album, Dex?"

"I did."

"And?"

"It's filled with old photographs and engravings and handbills. And, most of all, newspaper articles from a hundred years ago."

"Great," Frederick moaned. "Some antique-store piece of junk. That doesn't tell us anything."

"Actually, it does. The articles are all reports about a medicine show. Master Melville's Medicine Show."

"I don't understand," Esmeralda said.

"It confused me, too. A hundred years ago there was another Master Melville's Medicine Show. It travelled around giving performances and selling Hop-Hop Drops. It had a caravan that looked just like ours—I saw photographs. That can only mean that the Melvilles—*our* Melvilles, I mean—are imitating that old show. They've used the articles and the pictures to build an identical caravan. They make Hop-Hop Drops with the same recipe. They travel around with performers who are kids. What's more, they even travel to the very same places. There's a big folded map stuck inside the album, an old map, and it's marked with every place that the old medicine show went to, along with the date. I think the original Melvilles must have made the scrapbook themselves."

"So let me get this straight," Clarence said. "We've been kidnapped by a couple of lunatics who are pretending to be a medicine show that existed a hundred years ago. People who even changed their names. That's what you're telling us?"

"Pretty much. Except maybe for the lunatic part."

"But they must be crazy," Lilly said. "I can understand wanting to run a medicine show a century ago. But now?"

"Maybe they wish that they had lived in another time," Frederick said. "I might be crazy too, but I kind of get that."

Sullivan leaned forward on his bunk. "That's just what I've been thinking all these months. And in some weird way, it made me sympathize with them a little. I mean, if they're crazy, then it's not exactly their fault, right? They can't help it."

"But . . . ?" Clarence's word hung in the air.

"But it isn't true. They aren't just crazy. They actually have a reason for doing all this. A selfish, grubby, ordinary reason. I figured it out from the newspaper articles. A hundred years ago the original Melvilles issued a public challenge."

"What sort of challenge?" Lilly asked.

"They claimed that Hop-Hop Drops were different from all the other medicines out there. And they challenged anyone to prove they didn't work. They offered a reward. Five hundred gold coins."

Frederick whistled. "That must be worth a lot of money."

"The Melvilles said that they had hidden the gold coins while on their travels. It was a brilliant marketing strategy. The newspapers ate it up. People flocked to the show and bought tons of Hop-Hop Drops."

"So who won the gold coins?" Clarence asked.

"Nobody. At least, nobody did before the Melvilles got accused of kidnapping children to perform in their show. There were newspaper articles about that, too. And at the end of the scrapbook, somebody wrote a few words: *Too dangerous. Sailing for South America tomorrow.* The Melvilles—the original ones, I mean— fled the country."

"What a story," Esmeralda said.

"And the gold coins?" Frederick asked.

"I guess they were never found. Which means they might still be hidden. That must be what the Melvilles are doing. They must have found the scrapbook and read about the reward. They're following the route of the original show in order to find the gold coins. Gold must be worth ten times, maybe even a hundred times what it was worth back then. It's a fortune. That's why Monty is always hunting around, looking under rocks and down holes and inside old barns. He's searching for the gold coins."

"But why wouldn't they just go looking for it?" Esmeralda wondered. "Why copy the medicine show?"

"I know why," Frederick said. "Because they want to get inside the heads of the Melvilles. They want to think like them. That's the only way they'll be able to find the coins when nobody else has."

"Unless there aren't any gold coins," Lilly added. "The original Melvilles could have been lying."

"Then it's all for nothing," Clarence said. "But either way, Dexter is right. We're here because of greed. Simple greed. We're just a means to an end. We're here to help the Melvilles find the gold. It's just about money."

They sat silently in the dark absorbing all that they had heard, all that they were understanding now for the first time.

The key rattled in the lock. All of them froze, waiting for the door to open. The blinding light made them cover their eyes.

"Tonight's show is cancelled," Master Melville announced. "We're moving on."

"I have to pee," Clarence said.

"Is that smoke in the distance?" Esmeralda asked, looking out the door. "It looks like something's on fire."

"There's no time." Master Melville closed the door again, extinguishing the light once more. Sullivan heard Soggy Biscuit being harnessed to the caravan, heard the crack of the whip, felt the caravan begin to move.

"I don't know what's going on," Frederick said, "but it's not good."

FEAR

Nobody likes a depressing poem
Or worse, a verse that's without hope.
A poem should help us all to cope
Should hop, hop, hop, not mope, mope, mope.

So no more dreary lines for me.
Instead, my poems will sing with glee.
And none for you, O reader dear,
But rather only words of cheer.

So let us vow to seek and find
Joy in our lives (not just in rhyme).
What we yearn for, we shall grasp
Close to our hearts—at last, at last.

⬿ Published in the *Beanfield Gazette* ⬾

IT wasn't easy for Gilbert and Loretta Mintz to leave the Stardust Home for Old People, even for a few days. They had to find two trustworthy replacements (a nice couple named the Borregas) to watch over the forty-seven residents. Loretta had asked Norval and Samuel to drop in to help, but that didn't mean she wouldn't worry the whole time they were away.

And then, just as they were leaving, the Mintzes were stopped at the door by a representative of Beanfield Mortgage and Loan. The man, who had a bristly moustache, carried a calculator in his hand and a camera around his neck.

"I've got to go through the house room by room," he said. "Then I've got to provide an estimate of its worth—not just the house, but the contents, too."

"This really isn't a good time," Gilbert said.

"It's never a good time to go bankrupt, is it?" said the man. "And you're very close to doing so again, Mr. and Mrs. Mintz. Late payments. Insufficient payments. *Non*-payments. In fact, I'm surprised your loan was approved in the first place, given your dismal record. You will be in default in three weeks. Then the bank takes over."

"It's not just us you're threatening," Loretta said. "There are forty-seven senior citizens living here."

"Mrs. Mintz, I'm not threatening anybody. I'm just doing my job. This won't take long. I'm very good at it."

"Go ahead," said Gilbert. "The sooner you're done, the sooner we can leave. We have a train to catch."

"I'll be lickety-split," said the man, already pointing his camera.

❋

The Mintzes caught their train just in time and made it to Marsden, which was eighty miles from Fenton's Corners. They ran all the way to the Putt-Putt Rent-a-Car there, where the parents of the missing children were due to meet. The Samartinos had already arrived by another train. Ellen Raskin and Ann Whitford had come in by plane. So as soon as Gilbert and Loretta arrived, everyone piled into a rented passenger van.

Several parents wanted to drive but Emilio

Samartino won out because he was a professional limousine chauffeur. They talked excitedly for a while, but as the unfamiliar countryside flashed by, they soon grew quiet. They were all a bit nervous. None of them knew what sort of resistance to expect when they demanded their children back.

"Look!" cried Ellen Raskin. A tall wooden sign by the road read: *Welcome to Fenton's Corners.* Mr. Samartino turned onto Main Street and began to slow down.

Several people ran past them on the sidewalk.

Several more ran past.

A bell clanged loudly from somewhere.

"Is that smoke?" asked Gilbert Mintz.

"Something's going on in town," Mr. Samartino said. "I hope it doesn't mess up our plans."

Ann Whitford was sitting beside the driver. "They've blocked the street off up ahead. I see barriers. We'd better pull over."

At that moment a siren began to wail. The van pulled over and a red fire truck hurtled by. It braked before the barrier. Men and women in firefighting gear began climbing out and unwinding hoses.

"I don't like this," Loretta said. "We'd better find out what's going on." She opened the door of the van and got out. Gilbert came after her and the others followed. They gathered on the sidewalk, gaping at the flames licking up the side of an old building from the blown-out windows of the first two floors. Flames danced on the roof, too, and at that moment a section of the wooden roof fell to the ground, scattering sparks. Firefighters aimed their hoses onto the burning wood while others began cranking a ladder up from the truck towards the highest windows.

"That's the hotel!" Loretta cried. "That's where Jinny and Manny are staying!" She started to run and Gilbert followed. She called out their names but the roar of the flames and the clanging of the bell swallowed up her voice. They reached the barrier, where a man in a doorman's uniform was standing among the onlookers.

"Please," Loretta said, pulling at his jacket. "What about the people staying in the hotel?"

The man didn't take his eyes off the building. "We only had one room rented. They're up on the top floor."

"The top floor!"

"Loretta!"

But she was already pushing her way between the two police sawhorses. Gilbert hurried after her. They looked up at the same time and saw Jinny standing by the window, a handkerchief pressed against her nose. But they couldn't see Manny.

"That's my daughter! That's my daughter! You have to save her!"

A firefighter came up and gently pushed them back. "We're trying right now, ma'am. But you have to get behind the barrier. You're only going to be in the way."

Gilbert took Loretta's arm and led her back. They held their breath as the ladder on the truck cranked up farther towards the window. It came to within a couple of feet and stopped. Then a firefighter wearing full gear began to climb up. He paused halfway to adjust something on his belt, causing Loretta to utter a small cry of dismay, but then he was moving again.

"Come on, come on," urged Gilbert under his breath.

The firefighter reached the top of the ladder and motioned for Jinny to come towards him. But she shook her head, saying something and pointing inside the room. The firefighter argued with her, but at last he gave in and climbed through the window. He disappeared for a long moment and then reappeared with Manny over his shoulder. The old man was completely limp.

The firefighter struggled out of the window, turning Manny at an angle so as not to smack his head on the window frame, and got himself back on the ladder. He had to inch his way down. Loretta was crying silently now while Gilbert held on to her. But when the firefighter got to the truck and others picked Manny up and brought him to the ground, he couldn't contain her from pushing past the barrier again.

Meanwhile, a second firefighter was heading up the ladder. Flames could be seen leaping inside the room. Forced out by the heat, Jinny began to climb from the window. With a dangling foot, she tried to find the first rung of the ladder while she held on to the windowsill, but it was just out of reach. The firefighter hurried up, calling to her to hold on. He was ten rungs from the top, then eight, six . . . he was almost there when Jinny let go of the windowsill and fell.

The crowd gasped. As the firefighter caught her around the waist, the ladder trembled like a rubber band. He held her for a moment before they took a first step on the ladder. She was all right! She was on her way down!

Now Loretta and Gilbert rushed back to Manny. He was lying on a stretcher, with an oxygen mask on his face and a drip going into his arm.

"Is he going to be all right?" Gilbert asked.

The ambulance attendants lifted the stretcher. "Smoke inhalation," said one. "We won't know until we get to the hospital. It's in the next town, straight south down the highway."

"Can I go with you?" Gilbert asked. "Loretta, you'll stay with Jinny."

"Yes, please let him," Loretta said. "We're the only family he has."

"Sure, get in."

Gilbert climbed in after them. The attendant yanked the doors shut and the ambulance pulled slowly away.

Now Loretta watched as Jinny and the firefighter reached the ground. She clasped Jinny tightly and then held her out in order to make sure she wasn't hurt.

"Are you all right? Are you burned anywhere?"

"No, Mom. Manny protected me. Is he dead? Please don't let him be dead."

"He's on his way to the hospital right now. Dad's with him. What a terrible thing, to be trapped like that. These old hotels aren't safe."

"It wasn't the hotel, it was them. It was the Melvilles."

"What?"

"They came to see us. But I didn't recognize them. They were dressed funny. They came and then the fire started. I know it was them, I know it."

"We've got to hurry and catch them. Before they get away. We have to get Sullivan back. Come on, Jinny!"

She grabbed Jinny's hand and made her way through the crowd of people, back to the barrier where the other parents waited. But someone—someone large and wearing a blue uniform—stepped in front of them.

"Hold on there, please."

It was a policeman. A very tall, very wide policeman with blond hair and blue eyes. "You can't go just yet," he said.

"But we have to! They're going to get away."

"This is a crime scene. Somebody started this fire. You can't go anywhere."

"But we're looking for our children," Emilio Samartino said, coming over with the others. "If we don't hurry it'll be too late."

"You're all together? Then you can't leave either. Not until the detective says so."

"Where is he, then?" Loretta asked. "Let me talk to him so we can go."

"He'll be here. Might be a couple of hours, though. We've only got one detective in town and he's on another case."

"No, that's impossible. We can't stay. I'm sorry but we're going—"

Loretta felt cold steel on her wrist and heard a click. She looked down at her hand.

"Handcuffs? You're putting me in handcuffs?"

"Nobody," intoned the policeman, "is going anywhere."

✳ 22 ✳

OLD INITIALS

THE caravan rumbled on, its wheels bouncing on the uneven ground. The performers held on to the edges of their bunks.

"They can't work Soggy Biscuit so hard," Esmeralda said. "They're going to kill him."

"Do you think they care?" Lilly answered.

"They must be pretty afraid of something." Clarence's voice vibrated as the caravan shuddered. "But I can't think in this darkness."

"I might have a candle somewhere," Frederick said.

"You've been saving it? Well, come on. Give us some light."

Sullivan could hear Frederick rummaging around in his things. A match flared and then a candle flickered. In the yellow light he could see the worried faces of the others. "I agree with Clarence," he said. "Something important has happened. That smoke. And then telling us to pack up quick. I think that somebody is on to us. Maybe the police. Maybe one of our families."

"Our families think we're dead," Clarence said.

"Unless they don't. There might be somebody who doesn't."

"But even if you're right," Esmeralda said, "it looks like the Melvilles have gotten away."

"But it's something to hope for, isn't it?" Sullivan suggested. "That they might keep looking?"

Nobody answered.

Sullivan lay back in his bunk, trying not to mind the shaking. Did anyone think he was alive? His mother or father? His sister, Jinny? If anyone, it would be her, she was so stubborn. But maybe he was just fooling himself.

"Hey," Lilly said. There's something carved into the wall above my bunk. It's somebody's initials. *J.D. Age 12.*"

"There must have been some other kid before any of us."

"Can't be," Frederick said. "I know for a fact that I was the first."

"Can I see it?" Sullivan asked. He got out of his own bunk and went over to Lilly's, which was directly above Esmeralda. "Excuse me, Essy," he said, putting a foot on the edge of her bunk to boost himself higher. "Where is it?"

"Here." Lilly pointed.

"It looks awfully old," Sullivan said. "The way the edges are so worn and blackened."

Now Esmeralda looked too, followed by Clarence, who said, "But the caravan isn't old. Didn't you say, Dex, that the Melvilles built it to be an exact copy of the original one in the old photographs?"

"I was just guessing. But what if they didn't build a copy? What if they found the original caravan?"

"No wonder it smells so bad in here when it rains," Frederick said.

"Okay," Lilly mused. "So maybe this is the original caravan. Maybe we're living in some antique. That's kind of interesting but it doesn't help us."

"Any information's a help. Let's remember what we know. The Melvilles are travelling around, maybe in a hundred-year-old caravan, because they're looking for some gold coins hidden by the original couple. But so far they haven't been able to find them."

"Because they didn't hide them along the route," Clarence said.

"Yeah, because there aren't any gold coins," Frederick sneered.

"Or," Lilly said, "because they hid them somewhere they knew was safe. Somewhere they could always get to, no matter where they were."

"Is that some kind of riddle?" Frederick complained. "Because I hate riddles."

"Somewhere on the route but always with them," Sullivan said. "You mean, they hid them in the caravan."

"That's what I mean, all right."

"That sounds possible," Esmeralda said, "except that we've been living in this caravan forever and we've never found any gold coins."

"We've also never looked for them," Clarence offered.

Sullivan looked from one to another in the candle-light. "Well, let's start looking now."

Sullivan started first. Since he was standing near the end of the caravan, he began to run his hands over the slats of the back wall. He knocked on the wood with his ear close, although he didn't know exactly what he was hoping to hear. The other performers began moving about too, checking their own bunks and the nearby walls. It didn't take long before the idea began to seem less than brilliant.

"I can't find anything," Clarence said.

"You know what?" Lilly asked. "I don't care about any stupid gold. I just want to get out of here. I can't breathe."

Sullivan looked over at Lilly. She was standing between the bunks, running her hand through her bangs over and over. He could see the distress on her face and knew that being shut in so long was starting to get to her.

"Hey, it's okay," he said, moving towards her.

"It isn't okay! I need to get out of here!" She shifted past Sullivan and Esmeralda to get to the back door and began to bang on it.

"You won't be able to get it open," Esmeralda said gently.

"Even if you could, we're going too fast to jump," added Clarence.

"I don't care. Who has something strong? Like a screwdriver. Come on, somebody must."

"I have a small file in my tool kit," Frederick said. "But I need it."

"I'm not going to swallow the thing. Hand it over."

Frederick looked at Sullivan, as if to ask, *Is this*

a good idea? But Sullivan didn't know and could only shrug, so Frederick took out the file. Lilly snatched it from his hand, but instead of trying to get the door open, she dropped to her knees and began to wedge the file between the floorboards.

"What are you doing?" Clarence asked in alarm.

"I'm going to make a hole. And then I'm going to drop out of it. That way I won't fall very far."

"But you could get run over by the back wheels."

"Not if I'm careful."

Sullivan crouched down beside her. She pulled up on the file and splintered off a small piece of wood. Then she worked the file under the broken edge of the plank.

"Lilly, it's too dangerous."

"I can't sit around any more," she said, and she groaned as she put all her weight on the file and tore up a larger splinter of wood. "I'm going to get out of— darn, there's something hard under here. Look out, I've got it wedged in good."

Sullivan watched as Lilly jammed the file down with all her strength. A chunk of wood flew upwards, banging him in the chest.

"Sorry," she said. She leaned forward to peer closer to the floor. "What *is* that?"

"Freddy, move your candle closer," Sullivan said.

A short piece of plank had been taken out, exposing something smooth underneath. The candlelight gave it a soft, shiny glow. Sullivan reached down to touch its smooth surface.

"Don't tell me," Clarence said.

Sullivan lifted the shiny thing up. He held it in the palm of his hand for the others to see. "A gold coin," he said in wonder. "They're *here*. They're under the planks."

They stared at it and then looked at one another. And all were thinking the same thing. *What do we do now?*

VITAL SIGNS

GILBERT Mintz felt helpless as he sat in the ambulance while the attendant checked Manny Morgenstern's pulse again and replaced the bag of fluids dripping into his arm. They drove up to the emergency entrance of the hospital and a nurse opened the back doors for the stretcher to come down. They hustled Manny inside while another nurse told Gilbert to stay in the waiting room.

Gilbert paced back and forth, ignoring the television and the pile of old magazines. A half hour went by, an hour. At last a doctor came out.

"His vital signs are all good," the doctor said. "He did have some smoke inhalation, and there are minor burns on his hands. He'll be coughing for a few days, and we'd like to keep him here just to be sure. But he's a lucky man."

"Thank goodness," Gilbert said.

At that moment the door to outside opened and a young police officer came in.

"You need to come with me," the officer said. "You can join your friends down at the station."

"All right. I'd just like to see Manny first."

"As long as I come along."

And so the doctor, the police officer, and Gilbert went to the small room where Manny lay in bed with his eyes closed. Both his hands were bandaged.

Gilbert leaned close to him. "Manny, can you hear me?"

Manny coughed. He opened his eyes and smiled. "Gilbert. Is Jinny all right?"

"Yes, she's fine. Just worried about you."

"You tell her that I'm fine. Where is Loretta?"

"At the police station, where they're about to take me. They seem to think we had something to do with the fire."

"Officer, have them send someone to take a statement from me. These people didn't start the fire. I know who did. At least, I know who they are pretending to be."

"Yes, sir, I'll do that."

"Gilbert, I've got something you need." Manny broke into a coughing fit.

"Maybe you shouldn't talk any more," Gilbert said.

"It's . . . important. Look in my shirt pocket."

"If you say so."

From Manny's pocket Gilbert drew out a small card. "There are words crossed out on it. And a name. It says *Horfmutter.*"

"The other side. Turn it over."

Gilbert did so. Written in the same ink was *Fenton's Corners.* And under that was *Pooleville* and beside that *Sunday.*

Manny took several shallow breaths. "Pooleville is thirty miles from here. That must be where they're going next."

Norval Simick and Samuel Patinsky began to understand for the first time what Sullivan's life had really been like before the kidnapping. At the Stardust Home for Old People they helped the Borregas to serve the meals and clean up afterward. They folded laundry. They ran up and down the stairs delivering pills, mail, and newspapers. It was exhausting. But they also found out that old people were pretty interesting.

"You know what that Lucille Netterman used to do?" Samuel said to Norval as they were wiping down the tables after dinner. "She used to be an actor on the radio. Before TV was even invented."

"That's pretty cool." Norval nodded. "Mr. Harvey told me that during World War II, he had to jump with a parachute out of an airplane over France. While guns were firing at him."

Just then the telephone in the kitchen rang. Norval looked around but nobody else was about so he went to answer it.

"This is Gilbert," came the voice at the other end. "Who is that?"

"Hi, Mr. Mintz. It's Norval. We've been waiting to hear. Did you rescue Sullivan?"

"No, they got away. But we know where they're going, a town called Pooleville. So we're going to be away a little longer. Can you tell the Borregas?"

"Sure thing. You're going to get him this time, right?"

"I hope so."

When he got off the phone, Norval told Samuel what had happened.

"You know what they need?" Samuel said. "Reinforcements. We have to get out there and help."

"I don't know," Norval said. "How would we even get there? I can't just disappear without telling my parents."

"I guess you're right." Samuel scratched the top of his head. "But there must be some way."

"I've got an idea." Norval picked up the phone again. He dialled the operator and asked for the number of the Beanfield Police Station. But when he reached the desk, the policeman told him that the officers who had been in charge of the Mintz case were on their honeymoon in Niagara Falls. Norval thanked the officer and hung up again.

"So much for that idea," Samuel said.

"What do you mean?" Norval said. "All we have to do is phone every hotel in Niagara Falls. I mean, how many can there be?"

About a hundred and fifty, as it turned out, the falls being a major tourist destination. They took turns calling, hoping that the long-distance charges weren't going to be the final cause of the Mintzes going bankrupt. The first thirty-six hotels had no Spoonitch–Forka or Forka-Spoonitch, but the thirty-seventh did.

"Hello?" said a male voice.

"Ah, hi," Norval said. "You don't know me but I'm a friend of Sullivan Mintz."

"Of the *late* Sullivan Mintz, I'm afraid. I know we'd all like to believe different."

"But he *is* alive, Officer. And the Mintzes know where he's going to be tomorrow. In Pooleville."

"Listen, son, we've got just two more days on our honeymoon and my new wife is waiting for me on the miniature-golf course."

"I'm really sorry. But the people who kidnapped Sullivan managed to get away once. This could be the last chance. The Mintzes need help. And we don't have any way to get there, unless you take us."

"Even if I believed you, which I don't, it would take us hours to get back to Beanfield. And then we'd have to get to this Pooleville place, wherever it is. Ah, see? My wife has come back because she waited for me so long. . . . What's that, honey? . . . It's about Sullivan Mintz again. . . . Yes, a friend of his. Why don't *you* talk to him."

"Hey," said Samuel, "give me the phone." He grabbed it out of Norval's hand.

"This really is going too far," said a female voice.

"Listen," Samuel said. "What if it's true? And what if you not coming means that Sullivan Mintz and a bunch of other kids remain kidnapped for the rest of their lives? How would you feel then, huh?"

"Are you trying to make me feel guilty? That's not very nice."

"Madame Officer," Samuel said, "being nice is

not going to save our friend. Besides, I'm not trying to make you feel guilty. I'm trying to make you feel hopeful. We have a chance here to rescue Sullivan. Even if it's only a one-in-a-million chance, and I think it's a lot better than that, wouldn't it be worth it?"

There was a long pause. "Just a minute." She muffled the phone but Samuel could hear her speaking to her husband. "You know, honey, it's a really big falls but I've seen enough of it. Let's get packing."

* 24 *

THERE'S NO PLACE LIKE POOLEVILLE

THE caravan came to a halt. Sullivan sat up on his bunk, listening. He knew the others were doing the same. Had they really stopped for good, or just for a moment? Would they get to see the light of day again?

They had managed to pull up a big enough piece of floorboard near the middle of the caravan to reveal three gold coins. The coins were small but they had a nice feel and weight to them. Silently the performers passed them around before returning the coins to their resting place. They put the wood back as best they could, then covered the spot with a ragged piece of towel. This was a big secret and they all knew it, but what to do with the information was another matter.

Sullivan heard the key turn in the lock. Then the door opened, flooding the interior with morning light. Blinking, Sullivan saw the profile of Master Melville framed in the opening.

"Good morning, friends. I do apologize for such a very long confinement. But all our troubles are behind us. Do come out and take a breath of air. I'm sure you're all as hungry as I am."

One by one they climbed out. Sullivan squinted at the cloudless sky. They were in the middle of a grassy, rolling field—it looked as if some giant had shaken out the ground like a blanket. In the distance stood three granaries, tall and circular, with triangular roofs. One of them had words painted on the side: *There's No Place Like Pooleville.*

Master Melville was right about everyone being hungry. Sullivan and the others were eager to start a fire and set up the table. Master Melville himself made pancakes, flipping them in the air and catching them again in the skillet. He tipped them onto plates as soon as they were done, and they were just as quickly gobbled up. It was only when he was full and could think straight that Sullivan knew what they had to do.

He and Lilly were assigned to wash and dry the dishes. Working beside her, he spoke in a hushed voice.

"I think we should tell them."

"Tell the Melvilles? About you-know-what?"

"That's right. Tell them about the gold. That's what they're looking for. If we tell them, they'll have no more reason to keep us."

Lilly didn't respond right away but kept drying dishes. "Yes," she said at last. "I hate to help Frankenstein and his monster in any way, but it makes sense. And it won't do us any harm to tell them. After all, it's not as if we could spend the gold even if we wanted to."

"Let's see what the others think. We'd better be unanimous about it."

Clarence had fed the dogs as soon as they were outside, and now he was watching Snoot roll happily in the dry grass while Caesar ran in circles around her. Sullivan and Lilly approached him. As Sullivan had expected, Clarence agreed right away with his plan. Then the three of them spoke to Esmeralda, who was brushing down Soggy Biscuit. The horse was sweating and its head drooped.

"They've practically run the poor thing to death," said Esmeralda. "I don't think he can take any more."

"Maybe he won't have to," Lilly said. "Go ahead, Dex."

"I think we should tell the Melvilles about the gold. So they'll let us go."

Esmeralda didn't stop brushing the horse. "I don't know what to do, so if you three are convinced, I'll go along with it."

"Good. Can you leave Soggy a moment? We still need to get Frederick onside."

"Let me just get her another bucket of water."

They waited for Esmeralda, and then the four of them strode over to Frederick, who was sitting on a large boulder, polishing the shoes he wore in his act. By now Sullivan was aware that Master Melville was watching them closely. But they kept going until the four of them stood in front of Frederick.

"What's this about?" Frederick asked, looking up.

"We want to tell the Melvilles about the gold. So they'll let us go."

"You've got to be kidding."

"Do we sound like we're kidding? We want everybody to be in agreement," Lilly said. "So try not to be such a Frederick for a change."

"And what is that supposed to mean?"

"Oh, come on, you know what it means." Clarence sighed.

Esmeralda gave both of them a look. "Listen, Freddy. I want to go home. Every time someone tries to run away, it makes things worse. They've threatened our brothers and sisters. We don't know what that fire was about but it can't be good. We need to try something different. Let's give them what they want."

Frederick ran his fingers through his long hair. "Everyone thinks that I'm the bad guy."

"No we don't," Sullivan said. "We know the idea of going home isn't the same for you as it is for the rest of us. But you'll have to face that sooner or later. Let's all be together on this."

Frederick kicked at the grass. "All right," he said.

Esmeralda squeezed his arm. "That's good, Freddy."

"But I think Sullivan should tell Monty."

"Why me?"

"Freddy is right," Lilly said. "He trusts you."

"Wait," said Frederick. He looked embarrassed as he reached into his pocket and pulled out a gold coin.

"You're carrying that around?" Lilly exclaimed.

"I just wanted to know what it felt like. Take it, Sullivan."

Sullivan slipped the coin into his own pocket. He looked around and saw Master Melville pretending to examine a wheel of the caravan. He'd obviously been watching them but had thought better than to come over. Sullivan took a breath and looked at Lilly. She gave him an encouraging punch in the arm.

"Ow."

"Ah, go on."

So he walked away from them and towards the caravan. He didn't allow himself to hesitate but kept going until he was just two feet away.

"Ah, young Dexter. I didn't see you there. I was just inspecting the undercarriage. An ounce of prevention, you know."

"Master Melville, there's something that we want to tell you."

Master Melville tilted his head, trying to read Sullivan's expression. "Feel free. There should be no hesitation among goodfellows."

"It's about the gold."

Master Melville's eyebrows knit together. He looked harder at Sullivan. "I have absolutely no idea what you're talking about."

"You're looking for the gold coins that the original Melvilles hid."

"Nonsense. Why, I never heard of such a thing. Have you been reading *Treasure Island*? That's pure fantasy."

"Is it? Is it fantasy that you are following the very same route that a medicine show took a hundred years ago? That you're looking for the gold coins offered to anyone who could prove that Hop-Hop Drops don't work?"

Master Melville took a sudden step forward and, leaning over, put his face up to Sullivan's. "How do you know, eh? What nefarious trick is this?"

"It's not a trick. I figured it out. I read the album that the original Melvilles kept. In your quarters."

Master Melville took a step back. He put on a stiff smile. "I should have known that you would snoop about eventually. Yes, the gold. Take a walk with me."

"All right." Sullivan had to hurry to keep up with the man's longer strides.

"You see, Dexter, it wasn't easy to convince Mistress to marry me. But I made her believe that we would have a splendid life together. A life of wealth, excitement, and romance, free from the drudgery that ordinary people have to endure. And so she agreed. I was a salesman back then and believed that my winning ways were bound to bring us money and happiness. I sold everything from encyclopedias to bicycles, from televisions to tractors, yet I never seemed to get ahead."

"How did you find the old caravan?"

"By a stroke of luck. We were fleeing some creditors—very unpleasant people we owed money to. We left the city and hid in the countryside. But we had no place to sleep. Then we came upon an abandoned barn so I suggested that we get out of the rain and enjoy some rustic comfort. When I tried to lie down on the old straw, I discovered that something was buried in the pile. The caravan. Inside it was the old album telling the story of Montague and Eudora Melville. Reading about them in those yellowed newspapers, I saw an opportunity. Here was a way of starting new, of leaving our old identities behind. With my gift for selling, we could live off the earnings of Hop-Hop Drops while looking for the gold. Naturally, the idea of being on stage—even such a small stage—appealed to me. Salesmen love the limelight, you know. It seemed like a perfect plan. There was only one thing we lacked."

"Performers," Sullivan said.

"Quite. I restored the caravan and was trying to think of a solution when along came Frederick."

"You didn't kidnap him?"

"Certainly not. The poor boy was a runaway. Cold, hungry, and lonely. Mistress was particularly kind to him—she *can* be kind, you know. And he was excited to perform his magic before an audience. That was how we began."

"So you kidnapped the rest, including me."

"Kidnapping is a very harsh word. I like to think

of it as 'borrowing.' And we're providing you with an education the likes of which you could never get elsewhere. Look at you, Dexter, with your new act. You've reached great heights."

Sullivan said, "I suppose when you find the gold, you'll let us go."

"Of course. We'll have no reason to keep you."

"Do you promise?"

"My boy, I certainly hope you can trust my word."

"Because we've already found it."

Master Melville stopped walking. "I very much doubt that."

"Here, I'll show you."

Sullivan reached into his pocket and pulled out the gold coin. Master Melville took it into his own hand and felt the weight. He held it close to his face, examined it, and then carefully bit it. Then he looked at Sullivan and nodded. "Children are often better at finding things than adults. No doubt the rest is back at one of our previous stops."

"It's with us right now."

Master Melville looked surprised. He turned to face Sullivan. "Here?"

"Yes, here. They've always been with us. The gold coins are hidden under the floorboards of the caravan."

Master Melville slapped himself on the top of his

head. "Stupid me! It is literally under our feet. That makes perfect sense, now that I think of it."

"Don't you want to tell Mistress Melville?"

"Yes, of course. I would just like a moment to myself first." He reached out and patted Sullivan on the shoulder. "You're a smart boy. And a good boy, too. Loyal to your friends, true to yourself. And I will be true to my word."

Master Melville walked away. He hadn't yelped or jumped for joy as Sullivan had expected. Instead, he'd looked almost disappointed. Sullivan watched as he wandered about for a while and finally climbed up onto the caravan to enter through the small door behind the seats.

Esmeralda, Frederick, Clarence, and Lilly all hurried up to Sullivan.

"Well?" Clarence asked. "What did Monty say?"

"He didn't say very much. To be honest, he looked kind of sad."

"So what do we do now?" Clarence asked. "Just leave? Walk away?"

"No," Esmeralda said. "Not yet. I think we should wait."

And so they did. They sat or walked about, played checkers or cards, read a book lying in the grass. The late morning turned to afternoon and still the

Melvilles did not come out. Without talking about it, the performers began to make dinner. Clarence and Esmeralda looked into the supplies and came up with two cans of tuna fish, some pasta, a can of cream of celery soup, and a bag of unshelled peas. Esmeralda knew how to make tuna casserole. Lilly and Sullivan got the fire started while Frederick set the table.

Clarence said to Sullivan, "You're elected again. You get to tell the Melvilles that dinner is ready."

Sullivan sighed but he didn't argue. He went over to the caravan and knocked on the door. A moment later Master Melville put his head out.

"Dinner's ready."

"Ah, good." His voice sounded artificially cheerful. He turned and spoke into the caravan. "Dearest, it's time for the evening repast."

Sullivan turned and raced back to the others. "They're coming. Sit down, everyone."

The Melvilles approached arm in arm, Mistress dressed in her tightest black corset top, hair flowing to her shoulders, ruby lipstick glowing. They took their places and Esmeralda and Frederick served.

"Tuna casserole!" exclaimed Master Melville. "It reminds me of my childhood, so long ago. My dear departed mother used to make it."

Mistress Melville raised a fork to her mouth. She

hesitated a moment before taking the bite. She chewed and swallowed. "Yes," she said. "It's rather good." Esmeralda nudged Sullivan.

The rest of the meal was eaten in silence. At last Master Melville put down his fork.

"I believe a few words are in order. We have been together a long time—first the six of us and, more recently, with the felicitous addition of Lilly, seven. I, for one, like to think of us as a little family. Yes, I know it hasn't always been sunshine and roses. But don't all families have their difficulties?"

"Do make your point," said Mistress, although in a gentler voice than usual.

"Yes, well. Now it seems that you resourceful people have found what we have been looking for. There is, therefore, no reason for us to continue."

"Does this mean you're really just going to let us go?" Clarence asked. "No frying pans to the head, no threats, no punishments?"

"That is exactly what it means."

"Funny," Lilly said. "I somehow expected a giant fight or a chase or something. Instead, we just walk away."

"Indeed. But I would like to say something, if you would all indulge me. I will miss our life on the road, no matter how challenging it has been. The opening of the curtain, the glare of the torches, the applause and cheers. Watching all of you perform so beautifully. Already I feel a great nostalgia. Now, we may not deserve your sympathy or forgiveness. After all, we have stolen a piece of your childhoods. We have caused you and your loved ones much sorrow. Yet in time I hope you will look back with just a little fondness—"

"Really, Monty! You expect too much of them," complained Mistress.

"Yes, yes. But I would like to ask you all a favour."

"What sort of favour?" Esmeralda asked.

"I would like to do one last show tonight. A final performance. I think perhaps it will do us all some good."

Mistress sighed. "I should have known."

Sullivan knew his own reaction immediately. "Yes," he said. "I think that I'd like to do one last show. As long as we can leave right after."

"It's crazy, but I agree," Clarence said.

"I'm in." Esmeralda shrugged.

"Yes, me too." Frederick nodded.

They all looked at Lilly.

"Okay, okay. I'm not going to be the party pooper. Let's do it."

"Excellent!" Master Melville clapped his hands. "Afterward we shall all get in the caravan and drive into town. We shall drop you there and you can telephone your parents. I hope you will understand if we don't linger. Now, I think everyone should have a little time to reflect before the performance. And then let's give it our very best. It will be the show to end all shows."

OLD SAYINGS

AFTER dinner, Master and Mistress Melville walked arm in arm to the caravan, and Master Melville helped his wife up to the seats. They slipped between them to the low door and ducked inside to their quarters.

Master Melville turned up one of the lamps but the light was still dim. They sat across from one another on the old leather sofas and said not a word. At last he picked up the ceramic jug, poured a small amount of the golden liquid into the two mugs, and handed one to Mistress.

"To us, my dear," he said, holding up his mug.

Mistress Melville sniffed and then brought the mug to her lips. She drank it in one gulp. "And now?" she said. "Just exactly what are we to do?"

"What do you mean? We have the gold. At last we will be free of worries. We can have whatever we want, just as I once promised you."

"Strange how it doesn't sound as appealing now that we have it. Nothing against you, Husband, but I can't quite see us living a peaceful life of retirement."

"Exactly my thinking, my rosebud. I have been waiting to hear if you felt the same. I'll be happy in finer clothes, enjoying those small luxuries we have so often had to do without. But we have both grown accustomed to this life. The excitement, the travel, the thrill of the stage. And personally I don't see why any of that should stop just because we're rich."

"But you just told them they could go."

"My dear, I am a salesman. And a salesman's words are not to be considered mere facts. They are more like poetry."

"You mean lies."

"All right, lies. But Eudora, just think of what would happen if we let them go. Can you see the two of us sitting in some mansion reading magazines all day? Or lying on some beach? We'd get on each other's nerves within a month."

"A week, I'd say. Fine, let us continue the medicine show. But how do you propose to keep them?"

"By simply leaving the country, just as the original Melvilles did. The difference is they weren't smart enough to take the show with them. After tonight's performance we'll lock them inside and head to one of the ports. We'll get on a ship. We've got gold to pay our way and offer bribes when necessary. Just think, my heart's delight. We can tour France, or Spain! We can see the Coliseum in Rome or the fjords of Sweden."

Mistress Melville rubbed her lower lip. She reached for the jug and poured herself another drink, then picked up the mug and took a sip. "Then this is not to be the *show to end all shows*, after all."

"My dear, we are entertainers. For us, *every* show is the show to end all shows."

DRESSING UP

IT took several hours to convince the police that Gilbert and Loretta Mintz were nowhere near the hotel when the fire started and had no motive to burn it down. An officer telephoned the Beanfield Police Station and was told about the disappearance of Sullivan. He also heard that the case was closed, and as the parents were leaving, he told them they'd be better off going home and staying out of trouble.

The parents hurried to the rented van, but not to go home again. Instead, they drove to Pooleville. That town had no hotel, and besides, Gilbert and Loretta and the others didn't want to risk being found out. So they spent the night at a nearby campground, where there were some tents to rent. They had no cooking supplies so they bought a couple of buckets of fried chicken at a highway restaurant and ate it by a campfire.

When it was time to sleep, Jinny was glad to have her parents beside her, even though it felt strange not to hear Manny snoring. And in the morning, she had something to tell them.

"I had an important dream," she announced.

"My goodness," her mother remarked. "We must know what the dream was."

"In my dream, I had a big moustache."

"Does this mean," asked her father, "that you're really Groucho Marx?"

"I don't even know who Groucho Marx is. No, it means that we should wear disguises. Like the Melvilles used to fool us."

"That's an excellent idea," Mr. Samartino said.

He had noticed a nearby flea market and they all walked over to see what they could find. Jinny decided against a moustache and instead got a straw hat and a pair of glasses with no lenses in them. Gilbert picked up a fake beard and a cowboy hat. Loretta found a blond wig and a green raincoat. Everyone picked up something to hide themselves.

They drove in the van to the outskirts of Pooleville and waited for the sun to go down. The dirt road was so quiet that for a long time they saw nothing more exciting than a groundhog crossing from one field to another. But then, in the distance, they spotted a dust cloud.

"Maybe it's a tractor," Gilbert said.

"I don't think tractors move that fast," said Loretta. Indeed, the vehicle was speeding towards them.

Jinny strained to see as it got closer. "Hey, I think that's a police car."

The car slowed down and stopped some twenty feet from them, and two officers got out.

"We've been driving around for an hour trying to find you," said Officer Spoonitch-Forka.

"You've actually come!" said Loretta. "That's fantastic. Now they can't get away. But how did you know what town we were going to?"

"I told them," said Norval as he got out of the back seat.

"*We* told them," said Samuel, following.

Gilbert smiled. "I'm glad you boys are here. The more the merrier."

"I just wish Manny was here," Jinny said wistfully. "It isn't fair."

"Who says I'm not here?" grunted the old man as he got out of the car too.

"Manny!" Jinny ran into his arms.

"Whoa, there, sweetheart. Watch the bandages on my hands. The doctor gave me a clean bill of health, only I'm not supposed to run any marathons. Do you think I would have missed this?"

Gilbert and Loretta looked at each other. "You don't think this is going *too* well, do you?"

"I hope not," said Gilbert. "Look at the sky. It's sunset now. I think it's time for us to go."

"They don't have disguises," Jinny said in a worried voice as she looked at the police officers.

"We'll keep our distance," said Officer Forka-Spoonitch. "We don't want to tip them off. Are we ready?"

Everyone nodded.

They began to walk down the road, leaving the vehicles behind. They were a strange procession, led by a young girl and followed by two police officers holding hands. After about ten minutes, Ann Whitford suggested they begin to separate so as not to appear as if they were arriving together. And so they did, and when other people appeared along farm laneways, or riding bikes along the road, the parents intermingled with them.

"Oh my," gasped Loretta. "There it is. The real thing."

They looked at the caravan set up in a field. The two lit torches made the stage glow against the evening dark. All of them felt their hearts beat quickly. Jinny, of course, was the only one to have seen it before, but when she looked at it, she felt as if, until now, the caravan had been something she had only dreamed about.

They took up positions in the audience, Jinny and Manny on one side, Norval and Samuel in the middle, the parents keeping to the back, and the police officers hiding in a clump of nearby sycamore trees.

"But where are they?" Gilbert whispered to Loretta. "Where's Sullivan?"

And then a man stepped through the curtains.

THE FINAL CURTAIN

"LADIES and gentlemen! Dear friends! For, although we have never met, I consider each and every one of you a friend. Are we not all sons of Adam and daughters of Eve, all part of the same family?"

Master Melville doffed his hat with a flourish. "As the philosopher once said, *Ars longa, vita brevis.* Latin words of wisdom, dear friends, to say that great art takes a lifetime and more to learn. But on this humble stage tonight you will see a band of enormously talented young people, wise and skilful beyond their years. Why, I have not the slightest hesitation in calling this the greatest medicine show in the world."

As Sullivan stood listening in the wings, Clarence leaned over and whispered, "That's because we're the *only* medicine show in the world."

Sullivan shushed him.

"You may not be aware of it, but tonight is no ordinary show, my friends. No, it is the final curtain. The last show that we shall give together. After tonight, this noble crew of entertainers will scatter to the winds, each to his or her own destiny. So watch carefully, take in this special moment, this bright star of shining excellence, before it explodes in a shower of sparks."

At that moment, the Black Death, strapped into her musical apparatus, began to play "The Cowhead Stomp." Master Melville glanced at her.

"But I go on too long. It is time for the show to begin. Let me introduce to you a young man who shall one day take his place among the pantheon of great conjurors. I give you . . . *Frederick*!"

Sullivan could see Frederick holding a slim black cane as he waited in the wings opposite. He looked unusually nervous, but as Esmeralda pulled the curtain, he stepped forward and bowed with solemn grace. Then he tapped the cane on the stage, twirled it in his hand, and let go as it floated above his head.

From the back of the audience came a shout.

"Don't move! By the authority of the Beanfield Police Force I am arresting the two of you, known under the names of Montague and Eudora Melville, for kidnapping and other crimes."

A figure was running up to the side of the stage. Sullivan stared in disbelief. It was a police officer! And running up to the other side was another police officer! Could this really be happening?

"Matthew!" cried a voice from the audience. A woman stood up.

"Mom?" said Clarence. He ducked around Sullivan and walked onto the stage, peering down. "Mom? Is that you?"

"Matt, you're all right! I'm so happy to see you!"

Clarence quickly climbed down at the end of the stage and his mother wrapped her arms around him. At that moment another voice called out.

"Louise?"

And then Esmeralda too was jumping off the end of the stage, to be embraced by two women. This was amazing to Sullivan, but it still hadn't occurred to him that somebody might be out there for him. Not until a girl's voice called out.

"Aren't you going to come down too, Sullivan?"

It was his sister. His little sister, Jinny! She was taller

than when he'd seen her last, but even in the straw hat and glasses, he knew it was her. He was looking right at her and he still couldn't believe it. He hopped off the stage as Jinny took off her hat and glasses, and a moment later she had her arms around him and her head against his chest.

"I didn't give up, I didn't give up. And here you are!"

"I knew if anyone believed I was still alive, it was you, Jinny. And look how big you are!"

"You look different too," she said without letting him go. "Are you still my brother?"

"Of course I am! I'll always be your brother."

"And you won't ever disappear again?"

"Never."

And then he heard his parents, his own mother and father, calling out to him, and a moment later he was being hugged from every direction and kissed on his cheeks and everyone's eyes were filled with tears, but they were laughing, too. And then Manny, good old Manny Morgenstern was there, offering his bandaged hand to shake. But Sullivan hugged him, too.

"This is amazing!" Sullivan managed to say. "This is unbelievable! In fact, I can't believe it."

"Hi, Sullivan."

"Norval? Huh?"

Indeed it *was* Norval Simick. He had often thought of Norval, but he had assumed that his only real school friend had forgotten him long ago. Now they patted each other on the shoulder. But who was that beside him?

"Samuel? Samuel Patinsky?"

"Hi, Sullivan," Samuel said bashfully. "I, uh, want to apologize for bullying you in school."

"You've come all this way to apologize?"

"Yes. And to be your friend, I hope."

"This is blowing my mind!" Sullivan ran a hand across his forehead. "I can't believe you're all here. And we're really going to go home together?"

"Yes, Sullivan, we are," said his dad.

The audience murmured in astonishment as people tried to understand what was going on. The two police officers had a firm hold of Master and Mistress Melville.

"Hey, Dex," Clarence said as he came over. "Or do I call you Sullivan now?"

"Can you believe this?" Sullivan said.

"I know. But there's nobody here for Lilly or Freddy."

Lilly joined them. "Essy's parents explained that my folks didn't know about all this," she said. "I'm going to use one of the officers' cellphones to call. I can't wait to hear their voices! But poor Freddy, his uncle just didn't bother to come."

Sullivan saw Frederick lurking up on the stage, half hidden by the curtain. He couldn't imagine how Freddy must be feeling.

"He'll have to go home with one of us. I'm sure he could come home with me."

"Or me," Clarence said. "He looks so lost. Let's go talk to him."

Esmeralda joined them, and the performers went back up onto the stage. This time it was Clarence who was pushed forward, and he told Frederick just what they were talking about—that he was welcome to come home with any of them.

Frederick looked down at his feet. "I could be all right on my own, you know," he said.

"I'm sure you could, Freddy." Esmeralda put her hand on his arm. "But you're too young. It's against the law. And we'd all be so worried about you."

"They might just send me back to my uncle," Freddy said gloomily. "I suppose he has the right to me, or something like that."

Nobody knew what to say. Sullivan looked over at the police officers holding on to the Melvilles. The Master and Mistress had their heads down, and for the first time, they looked to Sullivan like what they really were—common criminals.

But a good criminal was able to think on his feet. A good criminal knew that when a plan went wrong, it was time to throw that plan away and come up with another one, fast.

Master Melville looked up. "If I might say something?"

"We're not interested," said Officer Forka-Spoonitch.

"Yes, I understand your contempt for me, Officer, and rightly so. But I think for the sake of the children— for the dear, needy children—we should finish the show."

"Pardon me?" said Lilly. "Are you making a joke?"

"Not at all. I believe it would give you all a proper sense of closure. It would help you to move on with your lives."

Frederick spoke. "It *is* our last show. Maybe it would be good to finish it."

Esmeralda said, "I'd like my parents to see me on stage."

Sullivan nodded. He, too, wanted his family and friends to see what he could do. So the five of them came down again and spoke to their parents.

The adults were quite surprised, and not easy to

convince. After all, they were understandably anxious to see the children safely home. But the performers were insistent.

Their next hurdle was convincing the police officers that they needed the Melvilles to do their parts.

"And what makes you think I want to?" said the Black Death, her mouth a grim line.

"Now, my dearest," Master Melville soothed, "I think it would be good for everyone. And you know how you like to toot and strum on those instruments of yours. Besides, it's the least we can do for these young people, wouldn't you say?" And he gave her a long look.

"All right. But I can't play music if a police officer is holding my arm."

"I'll be standing right beside you," Officer Forka-Spoonitch said.

"And I'll be right in front of the stage, keeping my eye on you." Officer Spoonitch-Forka pointed a finger at Master Melville.

And so, once more they took up their places, and began where they had left off. The surprised audience sat down again, as did all the parents and friends. Sullivan made sure that Jinny was right up front.

Frederick dazzled with his conjuring act, after which there was tremendous applause. The other performers applauded in the wings, too, and Frederick came off smiling.

Sullivan went on next. He had not felt so nervous since his first performance on the stage. How long ago that was, and how much had happened since! He knew that he was still a kid, and yet he had grown up an awful lot. He had been treated badly by the Melvilles—been deceived and misused and manipulated—but with his friends he had learned trust and loyalty and responsibility. And now his mother and father, his sister, Jinny, Manny Morgenstern, and even Norval and Samuel were sitting among the spectators as he became the homeless and hungry boy who gets his hat knocked off and juggles it in the air.

He didn't make a single mistake. But it wasn't just his technique that was perfect; his acting was precise and yet subtle as he evoked the homeless boy's emotions. The audience cheered. People stamped their feet and Samuel shouted, *"Woo-hoo!"* Feeling very strange but also happy, Sullivan Mintz took his bow.

Clarence came on next with the dogs. Sullivan wondered whether he was thinking about poor dead Snit, even as Caesar was making everyone laugh. And then he remembered that he had to help Lilly into Napoleon and ran around behind the caravan.

She was wearing her yellow leotard and waiting.

"I'm not going to miss this old box of junk," she said, stepping inside. "They probably ought to put it in some museum."

"Lilly?" Sullivan wanted to say something about what it meant to him that they had met. But no words came, and he was about to make some joke when she suddenly kissed him.

"We won't forget about each other," she said, and smiled. "I know it." And then she lowered herself into the automaton.

Sullivan felt as if his face was glowing. He closed the top and wheeled her around to the wings.

The person who volunteered to challenge Napoleon was none other than Sullivan's dad. Lilly played up the automaton's antics—ear wiggling, steam blowing, and finally the mechanical "*Checkmate.*"

After Lilly came Esmeralda in her tutu and ribbons.

"See! The piperope!" Jinny said happily to Manny beside her.

"You were right, my dear. You were always right."

As the audience applauded Esmeralda, Master Melville leapt back onto the stage. "And now, my friends, our show is almost over. I would like to thank the woman of my dreams, Mistress Melville, for sharing this adventure with me, from its glorious peaks to its ignominious end. My sweet, if you would unstrap yourself from those instruments and come join me on stage, I have a few last words to share."

Sullivan stood in the wings with Clarence on one side and Lilly on the other. Frederick and Esmeralda watched from the other side. Mistress Melville came up on stage and together she and the Master stood in front of the curtain. Her husband took her hand.

"I wish you all to understand," Master Melville said, "that we meant no harm to your children. Well, no *very* great harm. But still, what we did was wrong. Very wrong. Yet is it not true that together we created something unique and wonderful? I shall leave it for you to judge." Master Melville looked at Mistress Melville and smiled. "The truth is we had planned to make this not the last show but only a new start. Alas, we are clearly outnumbered, and so it is not to be. We understand that you believe there ought to be serious consequences for our misdeeds. However, we have other plans, don't we, my darling? And so we say to all of you, *adieu!*"

What happened next did not involve any elaborate trickery. There were no chemical flashes or smokescreens or magical disappearances. Master Melville simply pulled Mistress Melville back through the curtain. And then the two of them—a look of fear on Master Melville's face and one of fierce determination on Mistress Melville's—bolted into the wings. They pushed past Sullivan, Lilly, and Clarence and disappeared behind the caravan.

There was a stunned silence for a moment, and then Sullivan heard the male police officer shouting, "Stop! Stop right now!"

People began to move every which way. They bumped into one another, they shouted and waved their arms. Sullivan and the other performers came down from the stage. And then Sullivan heard hoof-beats, and a moment later Soggy Biscuit came galloping through the crowd with the Melvilles clinging to his back. Mistress used her riding crop on the horse and then on a few members of the audience who were in their way. The horse broke free and began to run through the dark field.

"Faster, you nag, faster!" cried Master Melville.

Officer Spoonitch-Forka grabbed one of the flaming torches. He began to run after them, even though he couldn't possibly catch a horse on foot. The crowd surged behind, the performers and their families among them.

In the moonlight they could see the silhouette of Soggy Biscuit as he rose up the gentle slope of the field, leaving them farther behind. Sullivan asked himself a question: Did he want them to get away?

After all, he and the others were now free. But then he remembered how the Melvilles had kidnapped them, and tied Clarence up in a cemetery, and kept Lilly locked in the Vanishing Box, and told them terrible lies about their families. He turned to Esmeralda.

"Essy, Soggy Biscuit will listen to you. Can you do something?"

"I can try," Esmeralda said. Then she put two fingers in her mouth and gave out a long whistle.

At the crest of the hill, Soggy Biscuit suddenly stopped. He reared up on his hind legs.

"Look!" Esmeralda cried.

Sure enough, Soggy reared again, even higher this time, and Sullivan watched as Master and Mistress Melville slid down his back, flailing about as they tried to hold on. Mistress hit the ground first and her husband landed on top of her. The horse shook himself, took a few steps away, and began to eat grass.

Officer Spoonitch-Forka arrived first, still carrying the torch, but his partner was right behind him and snapped on the handcuffs.

"All right, no more shenanigans from you two," she said.

Esmeralda hurried up to the horse. "Soggy! Oh, Soggy, are you okay?" Hearing Esmeralda's voice, the animal whinnied and trotted over to nuzzle her cheek.

Sullivan's parents ran up to him and each put a hand on his shoulders. "We're not losing you again," his mother said. Right behind them were Jinny, Manny, Norval, and Samuel.

Sullivan looked from one to another, and then he did something that quite surprised and embarrassed him.

He started to cry.

"I missed you too," Jinny said, squeezing him hard.

✻ 28 ✻

TWIRLING, JUMPING, SOMERSAULTING

IT was too late to make the trip home that night, so Sullivan and the others went back to the campground. On his first night of freedom he lay down in a tent, which was even less substantial than a caravan. Everyone was too excited to fall asleep, and besides, they had a lot of catching up to do. Sullivan didn't know how to talk about his own time away, not yet, but he was more interested in hearing about what had happened to everyone else.

He heard that for a long time only Jinny believed he was still alive, and that she kept trying to run away to look for him. That their parents finally allowed her to go on the road with Manny. He heard how the Melvilles almost burned down their hotel. And how Samuel Patinsky had regretted being so mean and had sought out Norval Simick. How the two of them were now close friends and had been looking forward to the day when Sullivan would join them—"like the third musketeer," as Norval put it.

❄

When Sullivan finally arrived at the Stardust Home the next day, he was greeted by a row of forty-seven old men and women, some in wheelchairs and others leaning on canes and walkers. They gave him a cheer, followed afterward by a chorus of coughs and wheezes.

If you have ever taken a long trip or gone to camp for the summer, you know how strange it feels to be home again. Inside, Sullivan looked in wonder at everything he had once taken for granted. Upstairs he went into his own bedroom and looked at the books and maps and souvenirs that seemed to belong to some other life. He saw his juggling posters. He went to his dresser and pulled out the bottom drawer where he had once kept his juggling equipment. It was empty now.

Sullivan's parents said that he could do anything he wanted on his first day back, but Sullivan insisted on helping in the home. He served meals and carried laundry and did all the other chores that he sometimes used to resent. Meanwhile, his mother and father and Jinny constantly checked up on him, as if to reassure themselves that he was really home.

It was during that first evening in the Stardust Home that Sullivan realized how tired he was. He went to bed early. But it felt weird to be lying in a bed that didn't rock with the movement of turning wheels. He became aware how *safe* he felt, with a comfortable mattress under him, a warm blanket and soft pillow, and, most of all, his family nearby. And then, even with so many thoughts racing through his mind, he couldn't resist falling asleep.

❆

On his second day home, Norval and Samuel arrived on the front step to walk him and Jinny to school.

"This feels so weird," Sullivan said. He walked beside Jinny while Samuel and Norval led the way, carrying their skateboards in front. Norval . . . with a skateboard?

"What feels weird exactly?" asked Samuel.

Sullivan thought a minute. "Everything."

What Sullivan didn't know was that the police had already informed Principal Washburb of his return. At the very moment that Sullivan had been waking up for his first day of school, the principal had been meeting with Mr. Luria, the gym teacher. The principal and the gym teacher didn't like each other very much, but somehow the question of Sullivan Mintz had brought them unhappily together. This time, Principal Washburb would make sure that those kids, Norval and Samuel, didn't make him look like some kind of villain, the way he had when he'd tried to stop the Sullivan Mintz Celebration Day.

"An assembly," Mr. Washburb had said. "We need an assembly to welcome Sullivan Mintz back."

Mr. Luria had his own worries. He had seen the medicine show and had failed to recognize Sullivan Mintz. He could only hope that Sullivan hadn't recognized him in the audience. *The bigger the reception for this kid the better*, thought Mr. Luria.

"We can have the brass band playing," Mr. Luria suggested. "And a banner. And confetti."

"Good. And I will make a speech."

"I'll organize the cheerleading squad. They've got a practice before school starts."

"Let's move it!" the principal practically shouted. "We haven't a second to waste."

Both the principal and the gym teacher leapt to it, only to smack into one another like slapstick actors in some silent movie. After they picked themselves up, they hurried out of the office.

When the school came into view, Sullivan slowed down. There it was, the red-brick building with the playground and the field. It had been a long time since he had been in a classroom. What if he'd forgotten all his science and history and everything else? How could he possibly catch up?

"What's that hanging from the top windows?" Jinny asked.

"It looks like a banner," Sullivan said. "Is there a school dance coming up? Or a big football game?"

As they walked closer the enormous letters on the banner became clear.

WELCOME BACK, SULLIVAN MINTZ!

Of course Sullivan could read the words, but he couldn't make sense of them. A banner with his name on it? At a school where nobody even knew who he was?

Jinny read the words out loud. "Cool," she said.

"Hey, Jinny, you can read!"

"You noticed."

Things got even more peculiar when they entered the school and found the hallways deserted. "Hello?"

Samuel called, his voice echoing down the hallway. There was nobody in the office, or the classrooms either.

"Maybe we should go home," Sullivan said.

"Come on," Norval urged. "Let's check the auditorium."

The auditorium doors were closed. Norval let Sullivan go first, and when he opened them, a roar of voices rose up. Then a brass band began to play. Up on stage the girls and boys of the cheerleading squad began twirling, jumping, and somersaulting. The band suddenly stopped playing and the cheerleaders began to shout.

Look to the right, look to the left,
Who's the kid we call the best?
Throw or pass, he'll do it all,
Let Sullivan Mintz carry the ball!

"Isn't that a football cheer?" Sullivan asked.

"Oh well." Norval shrugged as Principal Washburb took the microphone from a stand. "It's the thought that counts."

✳ 29 ✳
SUMMER PLANS

F OR several weeks the ownership of the gold coins remained in question. A request was filed from the Newfield County Prison by a couple named Herbert and Doris Lickerton asking for the return of the coins, "given that they were found on a vehicle owned by myself."

Herbert and Doris Lickerton turned out to be the real names of the couple who had kidnapped Sullivan and the others. Even from prison, they were devising schemes. But a judge dismissed the request on the grounds that the Lickertons had stolen the caravan in the first place. Then an unsuccessful attempt was made to find the caravan's true owner. Finally the judge declared that the gold coins belonged to the five children who had found them. The gold coins were sold and each child received seventy-two thousand dollars.

Sullivan instantly knew what he wanted to do with his money—save the Stardust Home from bankruptcy. But it turned out that Sullivan was not allowed to touch the money until his nineteenth birthday; until then it remained in a trust fund.

"Good," said Gilbert Mintz. "That can be your college fund."

"It won't be good if we're living on the street along with forty-seven old people," said Sullivan.

"Forty-eight, including Manny," Jinny corrected him.

But then something quite extraordinary happened. Loretta had been so busy that she hadn't even realized that her poetry book had been published. *The Sound of "Moo": Verses Pleasant and Unpleasant* by the Bard of Beanfield, Loretta Mintz.

She certainly had no idea that it had already become a bestseller. The publicity around the kidnapped children (covered by the local papers) certainly helped, but it was Loretta's poems that people liked. Maurice

Broome, editor of the *Beanfield Gazette,* was delighted to write and hand over her first royalty cheque. The Stardust Home was saved.

❋

Over the weeks and months that followed, Sullivan's life began to feel normal again—normal, but not exactly the same. There were a lot of things he didn't take for granted any more. Every morning he was glad to see his parents, and his sister, and the residents of the Stardust Home. At school everybody knew him now, and while Norval and Samuel were his best friends, he had other friends, too. His parents made sure he had time to just hang out.

For the first two months after returning, he didn't juggle once. Sullivan didn't even want to *think* about juggling. When kids asked him at school, he would make some lame joke about "feeling off balance today." But one evening, after his chores were done, he felt the urge stirring in him again. He didn't have any equipment so he went down to the kitchen and picked up three oranges. He started a half-cascade and found that his hands worked easily, as if they hadn't forgotten a thing. Then he tried to add a fourth ball and they all came tumbling down.

And so he began juggling again. Once a week he

put on a show for the residents in the dining room after supper. Manny would introduce him, and Jinny, who was learning to play the recorder, would provide the music, most of which she made up. His parents would stop cleaning up to watch. The applause and stamping of canes and walkers showed much appreciation.

And then there was the lunch hour when Samuel Patinsky shouted "Heads up!" and tossed one, two, three tomatoes at Sullivan. He had no choice but to juggle them. The other kids watched in amazement. Under the leg, over the arm, a three-hundred-and-sixty-degree turn. The whoops and hollers and table thumping brought Mr. Washburb on the run. He thought those troublemaking boys were starting some kind of revolution.

As for Mr. Luria, Sullivan never did say anything about recognizing him, not even to the gym teacher himself. Mr. Luria, though, was a lot nicer to him in gym class.

At first, Sullivan spoke on the phone to Lilly, Clarence, Esmeralda, and Frederick almost every day. Frederick had gotten permission from his uncle to live with Clarence, and the two had become fast friends. They tried to use their real names with each other, but it was no use so they stuck to the ones they had become used to. After a while he began to speak to them just on the weekends, and then every other weekend. He went to visit Clarence and Frederick, and Esmeralda came to see him once. Essy had found a farm near her house to take care of Soggy Biscuit, and she would ride her bicycle over every day to see the horse. Lilly was the farthest away but they did manage to see each other a couple of times. And then the whole month of May passed without him seeing or talking to any of them.

Sullivan learned to sleep in an unmoving bed. He no longer woke up wondering where he was. But sometimes he would lie awake for a while thinking about his days and nights in the medicine show. He would remember a certain performance, a particular meal, an old-life party. Also moments of fear, or cold, or simple homesickness. But it was all so quickly slipping into the past.

In early June, everyone around Sullivan began thinking about the summer holidays. Gilbert and Loretta asked the Borregas to take care of the Stardust Home for a few days so they could all go to the beach. But that still left a lot of time to fill. Jinny was thrilled when the Samartino cousins invited her and Manny to visit for two whole weeks.

Even though they were no longer in financial difficulties, Sullivan thought he should make some money, just in case. The home had its own lawn mower; maybe he could go door to door, offering to cut people's grass.

And then one day after dinner the telephone rang. "It's for you," said his father, handing Sullivan the kitchen phone.

"Dex?"

"Hey, Clarence." Just the sound of his friend's voice made him smile. "It's been too long. What's up?"

"What are you doing this summer?"

"Not too much. I had this idea of gardening for people."

"Well, I'm thinking of a job that's a little more fun."

"Cool. Doing what?"

"I'm going to run a show."

"A show?"

"A show that will travel to summer fairs. Only we won't sell medicine drops. We'll pass a hat. My parents have agreed to drive us in the van."

"What do you mean, *us*?"

"I've already got a magician and a tightrope walker. And, oh yeah, a mechanical chess player. All I need is a juggler."

"Are you serious? Spend the summer with you and Essy and Lilly and Freddy? Performing again? That would be fantastic. But I don't think my parents will let me . . ."

As he talked, Sullivan turned to see his mom and dad both standing nearby. And smiling. They knew! They already knew!

"Sign me up," Sullivan said. "I can't wait."

"Great. I'm going to call the others and tell them you're in."

"Let me call Lilly," Sullivan said.

"Sure thing. We'll start planning next week. Later, Dex."

Sullivan hung up the phone. A feeling of happiness spread all the way from his toes to the hair on his head. He went over to his parents and gave each of them a hug.

"By the way," his dad said, "your sister wants to provide the music."

"I think she's earned it," Sullivan said. And then he began to sprint across the dining room.

"Hey," called his mother, "where are you going?"

"Are you kidding?" Sullivan called over his shoulder. "I've got a lot of practising to do!"

* *

Once more I must express my gratitude to Lynne Missen for her support and sensitive editing. It's been a great journey. Thanks also to my agent, Marie Campbell. The manuscript was first read and commented on by two members of the home team, Rebecca Comay and Rachel Fagan.